# The Palace of Virtual Reality

## Charles Schwend

Published by
Quill To Book
Publishing

Charles Schwend may be contacted at:
www.charlesbschwend.com

Quill To Book Publishing may be contacted at:
www.quilltobookpub.com

ISBN 978-0-9966512-1-9

# Dedication

To my wife Dolores, with whom I have had fifty-four glorious years of marriage, and still counting.

Other Books Written by
Charles Schwend

<u>Dragon Dreams</u> – A beautiful young woman; An intimidating old man; An ugly dragon; A mysterious sword; A mythology from the dawn of time. All challenge the sanity of an unwilling young sailor selected to become the leader of a secret organization that is over two thousand years old. While stationed at an old Kamikaze base, he saves an old man, with a secret life, from a frozen river. His valiant rescue empowers him by ancient mandate, to become the Master of the White Ninja, a position he does not understand, nor want. The story is a tapestry of myth, love, danger and death. Dragon Dreams will capture an open mind in a novel of historical fact and mythological accuracy. This is not a book of martial arts.

<u>Words To Read, A Collection of Short Stories</u> – A colorful, insightful, collection of 23 memoirs, stories and one poem, based on recollection, legend and fantasy. The writings stem from Schwend's experience in the U.S. Navy, hobbies, family, and observing the world around him. Fantasy and a vivid imagination provide the mental stimulation for the remaining words to entertain an inquisitive mind. The short stories are from true memoirs, observation, whimsical half truths to full out fictional whim.

<u>Gulag #7, The Authorized Biography of Karl Lawrenz</u> - A gritty account of Karl Lawrenz from birth in Pomerania, Germany to his current retirement as a U.S. Citizen, living in Highland, IL. This book is about his life and internment in a Siberian Gulag (POW camp) during WWII when he was 15 years old. He nearly died many times from starvation and illness.

After WWII he continued to suffer under the harsh Russian rule of slave labor. He credits God for his life; his wife Inge for the happiness found in his life; and the U.S. for the quality of his subsequent life. Some memories are a little grey. Karl cannot be one hundred percent sure that all his recall is without error. Some may not be remembered for a reason, or a purpose.

The Magical Switch – Originally written for a poetry contest sponsored by Famous Poets Institute and won an Honorable Mention from over seven thousand entries. The poem was written for a bedtime reading to assist young children to overcome their fear of sleeping in the dark. The book illustrations were made by Nicole Dormeier.

The Keys - A collection of short stories that will entertain readers of every genre. Readers have acclaimed the stories as excellent reading. The Keys will be especially appreciated by readers that want to enjoy a short story, put the book down, and return at another time to start a new story.

Words, An Anthology of Short Writings - Editor of and Contributing Author.

A Dark and Stormy Night – Contributing Author

# Prologue

## Somewhere in Ancient Britannia

*Oh God, hear my words. Let me die now and not suffer for eternity. I do not deserve to languish in this insufferable hell of darkness and solitude. I have prayed for even the smallest spark of light to postpone the insanity that has befallen me. This blanket of blackest night has stopped time. I know not if my confinement has been days, weeks, months, years, or centuries. My powers have dwindled to nothing. I feel I am nothing more than a memory of a memory.*

*I was Merlin the Great. I had planned to create a world of peace and happiness, and now I am less than a grain of sand. How could have I been so foolish to let*

*Niviane, the Lady of the Lake, trap and imprison me in this inescapable black vault of rock? She was more beguiling than the sweetest flower until she learned all that I knew. How could I have known what her ulterior motives were, before my sudden betrayal suffered at her hands? Her sinister actions turned my heart cold.*

*Even now, knowing what I do, with my demise imminent, I feel my actions, my mistakes leading to my present confinement, would only be repeated. As I feel my remaining essence, from the smallest part of my being, slip away, I know that I will be no more. My only consolation is that my manuscript, holding the records of myself and that of all the ancient gods will someday be discovered. Everything about the gods and I, all the physical descriptions and details of mental psyche and design, recorded for the inheritors of the world to view. Maybe then, just maybe, our deeds and thoughts will again enlighten the world.*

*I am tired of my cruelly imposed existence, and must now relinquish myself to the eternal sleep. I ....*

**Chapter 1**

In a secluded rural New England mansion, an old man leans over an electronic control panel, his white hair long and unruly, talking to himself. His jerky body motions coordinate with a spastic speech pattern. High-pitch giggles and half spoken words heighten the scene of a mad doctor in a futuristic science laboratory. A tattered old leather bound book lay open, pages yellowed with age, on the flat platform before the wild looking venerable man. A twisted sinewy finger follows scripted code lines of information, while data is entered on a keyboard embedded in a soft-lit control panel.

His eyes pan over the room with proud satisfaction. The equipment resembles giant vacuum tubes ten foot tall, and glass drums fifteen-foot long rest horizontally on massive cradles. Humming control panels, computers, monitors, a row of wired containers that could be mistaken for old fashion caskets stand upright, and everything looking like it came out of a sci-fi museum.

Dials are turned and numbers keyed in on an array of panel buttons. Banks of digital readouts and sine waves on oscilloscope displays are monitored. A larger, more prominent button, marked *Review* is slowly pressed. A turbulent mist forms in an upright tube. Miniature jagged streaks of lightning crackle and pop through the cloudy mass.

From the misty cloud in the large upright cylindrical glass container, a hologram takes form of an elderly man, with stately features, intelligence and knowledge reflecting in his face. "Yes. Yes," screams the bizarre looking man standing at the control panel. He throws levers, and pushes more buttons with uncontrollable excitement. Then with hesitation, the button marked *Finish* is pressed. The mist slowly swirls, and then clears. In another horizontal glass tube, a more substantial image forms. Cloudy gas boils around the core matter reposed on a surface bed of white marble. A jagged leap of electricity arcs through the chamber, illuminating the room with a stark bright flash. A liquid mist gently washes away the cloudy mist, revealing the elderly man as a solid, humanly fleshed being. A light breeze blows from head to toe, drying the man. His forehead wrinkles and lips twitch. Thick black hair waves in the circulating air.

A quiet release of pressure emanates from the tube as a circular end cap, the door, opens near his feet. The platform bed slowly and quietly slides out on rails, exposing the naked man to the electrically charged atmosphere of the room.

The man at the control panel becomes ecstatic. Leaping to his feet he shouts out. "I did it, I did it. I knew it would work." Running to the prone man, he softly says. "Merlin, can you hear me? Open your eyes."

Merlin slowly opens his eyes and looks up at this wild looking man hovering over him. "Where am I? Who are you?"

"Get up. Stand. Let me look at you."

*I must not be dead. God is punishing me with this nightmare. I am still imprisoned.* He looks at his surroundings, trying to gather his senses, to orientate himself to this new challenge.

The insane looking man grabs Merlin by the wrists, yanks him up to a sitting position, then to his feet. "Look. Look at you. You are perfect."

"Where am I? Who are you?" asks Merlin again. "What is this language I speak and how do I know it?"

"You are in America, a country that was unknown in your time. It is the year 2016. I am

Professor Ambrose Hamlock. What you are speaking is modern English that was programmed into your memory, as you were being re-created. Come look at yourself. Look at what I have done. Look, look." He pulls Merlin onto a rotating turntable surrounded with tall mirrors.

Merlin stares at his reflection. *This wild man, this Professor Hamlock must also be a magician. My image is perfect.* Then Merlin inspects his reflection closer. A younger man reflects back then when he was imprisoned. *I am truly free.* Slowly rotating in the center of the mirrors Merlin realizes that this is the first time he has viewed himself with such clarity. His head turns to focus and follow Professor Hamlock, to study him. "You are a great magician. You have rescued me from my prison."

"No, not rescued, re-created. I have re-created you. Come, now we must clothe and feed you. Come with me." Professor Hamlock leads the confused Merlin toward a large wardrobe.

Walking past the working platform, Merlin recognizes his book on the gods and he from long ago, the script is faded on the yellowed pages. He carefully dresses himself with the oversized clothes provided, while keeping a suspicious eye on the old man.

"I did not know your desire for fit or size, so I went big for comfort."

"It is suitable," replies Merlin, then let himself be led to a large dining area where a table is filled with foods he does not recognize. Servers stand by, waiting to accommodate the needs of the new guest.

"We have many things to talk about, but that can wait until after we eat and you have rested," said Professor Hamlock.

"I would think I have rested enough. How many years have I been sleeping, waiting for my rescue?"

"Not rescued, re-created. Merlin, I have not rescued you. I re-created you from out of thin air. You are the first of many. The gods described in your book will soon follow you to the present. You will, of course, advise me on what positive attributes of the gods to enhance and what negative aspects need to be diminished. You will be my right hand."

Merlin did not like being referred to as a right hand, an assistant or a secondary to an authority, *even to one who did not rescue him, but re-created him. Yes, I must patronize this powerful magician.* "Yes, I can see I have much to learn from you, and I will assist you in your endeavors."

"Merlin you cannot realize how your words humble me. With our joined minds, we can accomplish anything."

**Chapter 2**

After eating his first meal in what might have been over one thousand years, and sleeping in what is called a bed, a most comfortable place to rest, Merlin feels he is ready for the first day of his new life. He has mastered the use of the washing facility, after several exploratory attempts and marveled over the clear running water. He finds clean clothing folded over a side chair and after a short deliberation, decides to wear the unfamiliar underclothing that appear to be missing arms and legs. He admires himself in the dresser mirror wearing what he would later learn was jeans and a white polo shirt. Brown socks and tan loafers complete his dress. He feels excitement over each new discovery. No cording is needed to secure the footwear, his feet just slip in. The self-rinsing chamber pot startled him as he depressed the lever opening the water channel. The downward escaping vortex mesmerized him before he realized its purpose.

Flint black eyes sparkle as he views long neatly trimmed black hair and moustache. He chuckles, thinking of how he nearly cut his nose trying to finesse the clumsy scissors while viewing his image in the hand mirror. His lean face almost cracks from a smile as he admires the trim body reflecting back to him. He hears a soft knock on the door.

"Merlin, may I come in?"

*Strange that Professor Hamlock would ask permission to open a door in his own house.* "Yes, by all means."

The heavy wooden door opens without complaint. "Ah, you're up and dressed. Your breakfast is waiting, and then later we will bring over the first goddess, Aphrodite. I will show you what is required to give life back to a god."

After a breakfast feast, Professor Hamlock leads Merlin to a large room filled with the electronic wonders that he had emerged from the previous night. Each piece of equipment is carefully explained to Merlin, what made it work and how to control it. Merlin is a quick study. Comprehension is instant with sequential logic filling in the infrequent gaps.

"Now, you can bring Aphrodite to life. You should not need any assistance from me," said Professor Hamlock.

Merlin, with the confidence of an accomplished sorcerer, begins the data input from his carefully written book, excited about his task at hand. His attention is so focused on the many details, that he does not notice the professor looking over his shoulder, watching every move, smiling, nodding his head in approval.

A hazy female figure of great beauty begins forming in the holographic chamber. With Merlin's quick control maneuvers, the form dissipates from the upright chamber, and a more defined body begins taking shape, her details more pronounced, in the horizontal chamber of life. Professor Hamlock rushes to her side to watch the finalization. The chamber end cap snaps open, with a soft hiss or a tender sssshhh, like a mother quieting a small child. A honey-citrus aroma fills the air. The nude Goddess of Love, Aphrodite, slowly slides out of the tube, cradled on the white marble platform. Her golden hair appears to be a life onto itself as it floats in the circulating air.

## Chapter 3

She is complete. She is beautiful. She is perfect. Her long eyelashes flutter and her full sensual lips twitch. A quick inhale produces a gentle cough. The naturally endowed face with softness and a complexion like that of a baby, momentarily lay still as if asleep. Her eyelids slowly open, and then stare at the wild-haired old man bending over her. His long white hair curtains the weathered face and roaming eyes that meticulously inspect every detail of her.

*Now, who is trying to enslave me to their desires? Why are they always old men who only have dreams of their youth?* A roll of her eyes takes in a room that is beyond her comprehension. "Where am I? Who are you and what do you want?" She did not resist as the old man assists her up from the cradle to her feet.

"Aphrodite, you are in my laboratory. My name is Professor Hamlock. I have brought you to the year 2016. Come with me to meet Merlin, and to look at yourself. Then I will clothe and feed you."

Aphrodite looks down at herself and realizes that she is not wearing clothing and being stared at. She asks in an apprehensive voice, "What do you want of me?" Another, older man is standing off to one side watching her with a critical eye. *I will take control of this situation. This is not the first time men have tried to take advantage of me. They are just men, and like all men, will be unable to resist fulfilling my wants and needs.*

Professor Hamlock gently takes her hand and leads her to a round rotating platform surrounded by magnificent full-length mirrors. Aphrodite is entranced by what is reflected. *I have never seen myself like this.*

"Do you like what you see, what I have done?"

"Yes."

"Merlin, come over here and tell me what you think," said Professor Hamlock.

Merlin's eyes are locked on Aphrodite as he trips and falls to the floor. His face flushes from embarrassment. He feels foolish because of his awkwardness. The pain from the finger abrasions brings his focus to the present. *They must think me an idiot.*

Merlin stands to walk toward Professor Hamlock and Aphrodite.

"Are you all right Merlin?" asked Professor Hamlock.

"Yes." Then he said. "Aphrodite, I have always read of your beauty, but seeing you, seeing all of you, numbs my mind. I cannot find the words to describe you." Bowing, he continues. "You have my oath of protection."

"Merlin, Merlin? I cannot remember anything of you. Were you a member of the House of Zeus? Should I remember you from service, or legend?"

"No. I was a magician in King Arthur's Court, not a god. My time was long after yours."

Professor Hamlock takes over the conversation. "Merlin, we cannot let Aphrodite get chilled." Then said, "Aphrodite, come and select clothing from our modest collection. I am sure we have garments appropriate for you." He leads Aphrodite down a long windowed corridor to a large ornate wardrobe, and then opens the doors to reveal elegant clothing and accessories. Aphrodite carefully selects a clinging jersey, white toga that emphasized her features. Delicate white kid leather laced sandals sheath her feet. Golden combs are chosen for her hair. A swift swirl of hands readies her hair for the combs. A practiced seductive smile almost brings the two men to their knees.

*If only I were a younger man,* thought Professor Hamlock.

*If I could only remember my spell for youth,* thought Merlin.

Aphrodite, confident in her assets and allure, decides to examine the possibilities in this place and time. "What manner of food and drink is offered here?"

"Anything you can describe or remember," replies Professor Hamlock. "My staff can prepare any food or drink from the dawn of time."

"Good. I would like honey glazed hummingbird tongue with roasted tubers from the river Nile. This is my favorite from Mount Olympus. Can your staff prepare this?"

Laughing, Professor Hamlock said, "Yes, anything your heart or mouth desires."

A gentle winning smile graces Aphrodite's face as they walk toward the dining area.

After the meal, a frozen dessert is served. *This food called ice cream is my new food of choice,* mused Aphrodite.

**Chapter 4**

Professor Jago Mundez lowers his binoculars. The grove of trees on the hill overlooking Professor Hamlock's palatial home gives excellent cover while he observes his academic rival. This position on the wooded knoll feels like a second home. Every available minute has been spent trying to unravel the secrets of Professor Hamlock.

*If I cannot penetrate Hamlock's stronghold to take his secrets, I will have to dispatch him in his university office. With him out of the way, I will leisurely study his papers and equipment that he mumbles about while dozing at his desk. Maybe I can forge a will to become his executor and lay claim to his estate. The will would not be contested. He has never admitted to having relatives in response to my carefully crafted questions. With him out of the way, I will become the Head of the*

*Science Department. I still do not understand how that doting old fool was selected instead of me.*

Mundez steadies his binoculars as a beautiful nude woman, Hamlock and a strange looking man walk past the laboratory corridor windows. The woman was revealed from head to toe through the tall glass. His stare is focused on the woman, he breathes a little heavier and feels his mind slowly turn to mush. *Now where did she come from? No vehicles have pulled up while he was keeping watch. What's that crazy old pervert up to with that young girl? And what's up with that other old pedophile? Tomorrow, tomorrow, he is going to permanently retire!*

The next morning, Professor Hamlock sits at his massive desk constructed from narrow strips of Redbud wood. The exposed surfaces glowed from centuries of polish and loving use. It was a legend in his past family, its origin unknown. Vegetables from his garden are arranged in front of him on the desk for lunch. He attributes his longevity to being a vegetarian for the past thirty years. A knock at his open door breaks his train of thought. "Professor Mundez, please come in. What a pleasant surprise. How is your heart? I have heard that you are taking medication for it."

"Ambrose, my heart is fine. It just needed a little tune up. By the way, I came across this new tea blend and I just know you would die for a cup of it. I prepared it the way I know you like your tea – heavily steeped, one lump of sugar and steaming hot."

"You are just too kind." Pushing aside the bowls of vegetables, to make space on his desk, he said, "Please, set it down here." Leaning over he took in the sweet aroma. "It reminds me of lotus blossoms. Is that the main ingredient?"

"Oh no, the blend is a secret. Finish the cup, and then tell me what you think."

"This is fabulous. You must tell me what it's made of. To taste this good, it must be bad for you."

"Yes. Finish it and tell me if you can identify the ingredients."

Setting the cup down, Professor Hamlock stares into Mundez's eyes, "It – it tastes heavenly. I have never had tea quite like…" His head falls to the desktop with a dead thump.

"Yes. Heavenly isn't it!" Mundez stands up, walks to the door and after placing a sign, "*In Conference - Do Not Disturb*" on the outside doorknob, locked it. Leaning Hamlock's torso against the back of his chair, Mundez conducts a thorough search of drawers and cabinets. He finds nothing new. With a repulsed expression, he diligently searches Hamlock's pockets, pulling out his key ring. No keys to a secret site are found and he returns the key ring to the pocket. He looks around, checking again for any missed hiding space. Finding none, he places the teacup and saucer with the spent tea bag into a plastic shopping bag pulled from his coat pocket. After wiping down every surface that he might have touched, he presses his ear to the door checking for the sound of footsteps. Hearing none, he leaves, locking the door behind him.

## Chapter 5

Worried, since Professor Hamlock has not returned home for several days, Merlin feels relief as he hears the driveway bell ring announcing an arrival. He stands by the door to welcome him home. A knock on the door brings a puzzled look to Merlin's face. Opening the door, he finds a stranger. "Yes, how can I help you?"

"I am Professor Mundez, a colleague of Professor Hamlock. He has recently passed away and I am his only heir. I have a copy of his will. Now, who are you and what is your business in this house?"

"May I see your copy of the will?" Merlin looks deep into the visitor's eyes and sees a heinous soul. He holds out his hand.

"Again, who are you and what is your business here."

Merlin gives no reply, but stands with outstretched hand.

*I guess I'll have to hand over this copy of the will just to get rid of this leech.* "Here, now please step aside so I may enter. I will want a detailed inventory of the entire estate, before the probate hearing, to ensure everything remains here." Walking into the dining room, a server approaches Mundez with a questioning look at Merlin. "You there, bring me a drink. A brandy if you will."

Merlin sits across the table from Mundez and starts reading the will. His eyes fix on the date of the will. The day Hamlock stayed home to instruct Merlin how to use the equipment to re-create Aphrodite. Ripping the will into pieces and letting them fall to the floor, he said, "Sir, this document is fraudulent. The household staff and I can attest to the fact that Professor Hamlock was in this house the entire day of that will's date." *I might be old, but I am not stupid.* "Professor Hamlock has an only relative, a niece, who I feel will inherit his estate without contest. She will be saddened to hear of his death." Mundez's face flushes red with anger. Merlin continued with sternness. "Now, I must ask you to leave so I may make inquiries and proper arrangements." Merlin watches Mundez as he stomps out. Squealing tires signals his departure. *I must make calculations. I have much to do.*

Turning toward the laboratory, he calls out, "Aphrodite, come, we have work."

## Chapter 6

Leaving the rows of eye candy, Travis steps out of the 'Science and Inventors Source' store into the drizzling rain. The large selection of laser splitters confuses him. *I'll have to discuss any possible purchase with Austin and Dyllan. They are the geek guru's of the university. Unlike my interest in holograms and computer generated progressive visuals; they are into that boring rocketry and quantum physics.*

Flipping open his one hundred and ninety nine channel Black Apricot multi function smartphone, Travis pushes the pulsating icon of Austin's face. The cordless ear bud sounds the connection buzz to Austin's identical unit. Seconds pass before Austin answers. "Yah, speak to me."

"Austin, it's me, Travis. Hey, what laser splitter should I buy? This place you sent me to has fifty different models in stock."

"How much money do you want to spend genius?"

"As little as possible," said Travis.

"Yah, that's what I thought tightwad. Then get the multi channel wave gerder unit. It won't burn out when put on indefinite auto loop."

"Hey, remember Nicole's uncle, Professor Ambrose Hamlock? He died mysteriously and the police are still investigating. Nicole called. Since he did not have a will and she is his only living relative, she gets everything. She heard at the university, that his house is packed with neat electronic equipment. Tomorrow morning is Saturday, and we're picking up Nicole at her house to go to the professor's old place and check it out."

## Chapter 7

Waiting impatiently, Nicole stands tapping her toe on the curb. Austin leans over the front seat and opens the passenger side door as Travis comes to a screeching stop. "Come on, hop in."

"Where the hell have you been?" Nicole asks Travis.

"I had to wait for Austin and Dyllan. He was in a daze, stumbling around his place, and Dyllan couldn't decide on what to wear. What kind of place are we going to?"

Nicole turns to the back seat giving Austin and Dyllan a disapproving look through narrowed eyes. "I was only there once. Last summer he invited me out for a BBQ, but it was eerie. I never got into the house. I even had to use an old creepy, smelly outhouse that was bug infested. He said the house was being remodeled and in a mess. He did not want to see me get hurt, tripping over building materials sitting around. But I did hear some really strange noises coming from inside the house. He said the TV was on. It sounded to me like people were inside talking. That was kind of spooky. The place is a bit out of the way, rather hidden away would say it better. I think we can figure everything out once we see what's out there."

"There's the turn, into that alley looking lane to the right, into the woods on the curve," blurted Nicole.

"Damn, I would have missed it. I didn't see it coming up," said Travis.

"Yah, that's what I said; hidden away," said Nicole with smugness in her voice.

Austin yells out from the back seat, "Hey, take it easy on the snappy turns, will ya."

Dyllan giggled, "Austin, you're a nerd."

They enter a broad stone gate, and on the right pillar, "Hamlock Manor" was chiseled in a large stone block, embedded high in the wall.

"Holy crap, look at that huge palace," exclaimed Austin. "It looks like something out of an Adams Family or Disney movie."

Travis stops the car in a circle driveway next to

granite steps leading up to a massive stone porch and entrance. "OK, everyone out. Nicole, I hope the power is still on?"

"It should be," said Nicole. "Austin, bring that back pack with the flashlights, just in case."

Reaching the front door that looks like it came off a castle, with huge vertical boards, wrought iron hinges and bracings, Nicole put the large bronze key that she got from the probate lawyer into the lock. The turning key produces a scraping noise, unlocking the door. Just like in horror movies, the door screeched and groaned in protest, as it was forced open. Looking through the misty air reveals a large entryway with two stairways arching up from the sidewalls, meeting at a wide landing on the second floor. The floor is made of heavily veined marble, joints so tight it looks solid. It was obvious that pains were taken to match up the marbling veins. Paintings and masks of ancient gods hang on the walls. Walking toward the stairs their footsteps sound hollow and echoes through the great room.

Nicole reaches out and turns an old circular light switch. It did not work. "Austin, pull out some flashlights," commanded Travis. Four round spots of light explode out through the opaque air, randomly moving through the room.

"It would be awesome living here," said Dyllan.

Open mouths silently express, ooohhs, aahs, and sweet, below wide excited eyes. "Where do we go first Nicole?" asked Travis.

"I don't know, maybe up those stairs," whispers Nicole. With slow deliberate steps, the four quietly ascend the grand stairway, made of mahogany, inlayed with brass, and with a regal red stair runner emblazoned with golden laurel.

The focus of their lights move up the stairs to the landing, where the beams of light reveal three doors, one to each side of the landing, and the largest, directly in front of them.

## Chapter 8

Entering the room, Travis asks in a whisper, "Maybe we should split up to find the professor's equipment, and we could meet up back here?"

"Not on your life," said Dyllan. "We're sticking together. I don't care what you think. We're all sticking together."

"O.K., O.K., chicken. Everyone, just keep looking for…"

A loud reverberating voice engulfs them, "Good morning Nicole."

"Who said that?" whispers Austin.

"My name is Merlin. Master Hamlock put me in charge before he left."

"How do you know my name?" said Nicole, with a whimper.

"Oh, I know all your names. They were put into my… they were told to me some time ago by Master Hamlock, and I have held them in my memory. I believe that everything to be known is in my memory."

"Where the hell are you? You're scaring the girls. Come out so we can see you," stutters Travis. A sparkling swirl and a bright flash blind the four. When their eyes open, a tall regal, ramrod straight, bearded, butler looking man, stands before them.

"I am Merlin. Welcome to Merlin's house," he said with an arching sweep of his hand. "Come with me so I may show you the wonders of my home."

"Who else lives here Merlin?" asked Travis.

"There are many who live here, but not all at the same time. Aphrodite is here now and many others will come as needed," answered Merlin.

"What, this place is like a boarding house? Those people just live here when they want to drop in? And what do you mean, 'they will come as needed'? Uncle Hamlock has never mentioned any of this to me. And why are you in charge of everything? Why you and not me?" said Nicole.

"Because I am Merlin," said Merlin. "Come, I will show you the wonders of the house."

Merlin walks through the door where the group first entered the room then descends the staircase.

Turning at the bottom of the staircase, he opens a large ornate set of double doors into a large library. The furniture consists of large reading tables, sofas of different styles, and easy chairs of every kind. Paintings and collectables cover the walls not hidden by bookshelves. A Greek reclining bench is angled in front of a huge, walk-in fireplace. A beautiful woman rests on the arm, reading a book. At first it appears she is wearing night clothing, but when she stands up the cloth loses their drape and becomes semi-transparent, like sheer silk and lace. It is only when she speaks that Travis's mesmerized stupor is broken, and he realizes she has waist length wavy blonde hair, green eyes, and a figure that could only come out of a computer's paint shop.

"What are you reading Aphrodite?" asked Merlin.

"What else, Birth of a Goddess." She leans over to set down the old leather bound book on an end table, and then stands straight replying, "And who are your four friends?"

"This is Nicole, the niece foretold by Master Hamlock, and her three friends."

With a wicked smile that could melt chocolate, or anything else that viewed it, Aphrodite slowly said, "Oh them, which one is mine, Merlin?"

Merlin scowls. "None are yours. Now behave yourself or be sent to the memory room. Return to your book. We will talk about this later." Aphrodite again leans over the table to pick up her book. The flimsy sheer gown gapes open, leaving nothing to the imagination. She turns her torso to offer the maximum effect. Her face is angled, lips slightly parted. Her penetrating eyes focus on Travis, and the smile is more than inviting.

Merlin turns to his four followers, "Come, we will investigate the game room." Walking to a small alcove between bookshelves, he opens a heavy wooden door, and walks into a large room filled with electronic equipment. The four follow Merlin stiffly, not really understanding the conversation that just took place.

Nicole closes a gaping mouth, then asked, "Merlin, who was that woman and what was her relationship with Uncle Ambrose?"

"Master Hamlock gave Aphrodite life. He used this equipment that he designed and built. Master Hamlock created everything here," Merlin said with a smile on his face and a graceful flourish of his hand.

Austin, who just now came to his senses, surveys the contents of the room. The equipment is a wishful dream to a scientist and a nightmare to an electronic engineer.

Nicole's face reflects a lack of understanding, and asks, almost inaudibly, "What do you mean, he created everything here? What do you have…?"

"Master Hamlock was semi-retired from the university science department. When he could no long divert inquiring questions from rival professors, he built this equipment, and then with it, made everything here," explained Merlin, as if his explanation was perfectly normal.

"Well, is Aphrodite real? Is this all real? What the hell is really going on here? Is someone or something going to jump out and yell – You're on Candid Camera or some other reality show?" asked Dyllan in a high screechy voice.

Merlin gives Dyllan a cold, but understanding look and said, "Anything can be built in the game room. Some inanimate items built are solid, like the furniture, others are from living holograms that have substance, like Aphrodite. She looks and feels real. In essence, she is real. She thinks, speaks, and breathes, everything a real woman does."

"Yah and she looks a lot better than real," murmurs Austin.

## Chapter 9

"What kind of dribble is that, a solid hologram? There is no such thing. You and Aphrodite, if those are your real names, have a lot of explaining to do. I think you two are a couple of parasites that moved into my uncle's house. I'm calling the cops. You two belong in the loony bin. You're not right in the head," exclaimed Nicole.

"I told you that in all respects we are real, and as Austin commented, better than real. I am to show you all that is here, and teach you the ethics that constrained Master Hamlock."

A stunning red headed woman enters the room carrying a tray of sandwiches followed by an elegant man carrying drinks. Merlin gestures to the table when the trays are set down. "I took it upon myself to have lunch prepared. I am sure you will enjoy it. The kitchen staff is well versed in timeless and universal cuisine. Come and sit down."

Austin picks up a sandwich with an inquisitive look and sniffs it, "What are these? I've never seen anything like this. It isn't meat. What is it?"

"Taste and tell me what you think it is," said Merlin.

Dyllan had already picked up and opened a sandwich, running her finger through the pureed substance on the lightly toasted bread, put a bit to the tip of her tongue. "Oh my lord, this is good." Taking a bite she mumbles, trying to talk with a full mouth, "Hmmm, ohn tes brehd ith deevien." Swallowing the food with a gulp of water, she finally gets her voice back. "What is that? And that bread is not made from wheat flour. That is out of this world."

Merlin smiles. "More so than you might think. Our staff is very imaginative, referring to recipes that go back to the beginning of time. Now let us finish our lunch and return to our studies."

"I don't understand how this works," said Travis. "I know how a hologram is made, but how do you make it with substance?"

Merlin stares at Travis with a look of concentration, and then said, "Think of how an audio speaker compresses particles in the air, making them move, even to blow out candles or break glass.

Now think of amplifying the process even more, packing the particles until they solidify with the same ratio mix that matches your human body, duplicating your DNA, and then energizing the bio mass to bring life, and charging the brain mass with electrical impulses to create memory. Does this give you a basic understanding of the process?"

"I think so," replied Travis slowly.

"Can I make money, diamonds, or anything I want?" asked Austin.

"Yes," replied Merlin. "But only if it is needed for the better good. There will be some leeway for experimentation during your training period. This room is like a Genie in a bottle that can fulfill your every wish. You must know what you are really wishing for. But first, you must master the equipment. You must learn how the processes work. If you do not understand the process, or know how the equipment works, the end result could be disastrous for both you and what you create. While testing the equipment, Master Hamlock made a creature that was almost not neutralized. He corrected those errors. Now there are built in safeguards, implemented to prevent most errors, but then nothing is completely safe. There is always a possibility of a creation turning against its creator because of faulty reasoning."

"You mean like Aphrodite? She seems a little dangerous to me," said Nicole.

"No," responded Merlin carefully. "Aphrodite is a safe re-creation. She has what I would call expanded needs that befit the identity of her molecular blueprint. You are safe with Aphrodite, Nicole."

"How about me, am I safe near her?" asked Austin.

"You and Travis are a different matter. Aphrodite will pursue one or the other, or maybe both of you, but neither of you will come to harm. I should warn you, or any male in the house, to be careful of what you say, or what body language you project. You do not want to encourage her mythological calling. Now, meals have been prepared, and then we will start the enlightenment process. This evening, after supper, we will relax in the library, to discuss what we have learned, and what we will learn in the future. Please follow me to the dining room for lunch. Your favorite meals have been prepared."

Merlin escorts his four guests to the dining hall. We were seated, and formally served by women that could have been beauty contestants. They were all very professional, personable, but not personal. Questions asked of them were answered with a simple yes or no, and they would not engage in conversation. Austin was inquisitive, trying to get their names, asking where they live, their telephone numbers and interests.

A truthful smile was given to each question, but no answers. Dyllan is furious, and Nicole looks as though she feels a little outclassed, much like her demeanor when meeting Aphrodite.

Merlin noticing their distress said, "Do not be concerned over the servants. Their physical features far exceed their mental capacity. They were created to be servants, not functional in any other way."

## Chapter 10

Austin's facial expression reveals a complete collapse of libido. Turning his attention from the servers, he finally becomes aware of the lavish food placed in front of him. Relaxing, his attention becomes focused on filling his stomach. Austin gorges himself. Travis eats his meal while trying to observe everything, leaving much food untouched when the servers remove the dinnerware. Dyllan picks at her food, pushing most of it around on her plate except for the salad. Nicole consumed only the soup.

Merlin sits at the head of the table, obviously enjoying his role as head of the house. He nods to the headwaiter, and wine is served. Many of the questions from the four go unanswered, as Merlin, apparently, is a master of evasive conversation. He glances around the table, taking in the drowsy eyes. "Shall we retire, and continue our explorations tomorrow morning? Beds have been turned down, baths drawn, and suitable night clothing provided."

Dyllan replied, "But we are not prepared to stay overnight. We did not bring anything."

"Everything has been provided. If you find anything lacking or a need for additional items, ring for service and it will brought to your room," said Merlin.

Each of the four is escorted to their own lavishly furnished and enormous suite. The rooms far exceed their fantasies. It was as if Merlin had read their most private thoughts. All have their own individual spacious, state of the art, multi-head surround showers with steaming water, soaps and body lotions of every kind, and luxurious heated towels and robes. Personal hygiene products were laid out on the bathroom counters. Everything needed was provided.

Travis plops down onto his bed. Surveying the opulence of the room, taking in the canopy above him, the large plasma screen TV on the wall, the polished wood floor and doors, then thinking, *this is all made up. None of this is real. How could this be? Merlin's explanation does not really convince me.* Deep in analyzing Merlin's possible motives, Travis does not notice his bedroom door slowly open and a scantily clothed woman enter.

"Travis. I am here."

With the effects of the horror film atmosphere heavy on his thoughts, Travis feels like he is having a heart attack. Leaping to his feet, he turns. "Aphrodite. What are you doing here?"

Aphrodite stands as if modeling sleepwear on a runway, more revealing than before. "I came to check your bath, to see if it was properly prepared. Good help is hard to find and keep. I'll just check and be on my way."

Aphrodite reaches the bathroom door before Travis can stop her. The door shuts and locks. "Aphrodite, open this door," he shouts.

"Soon, just wait. I will not be long," replied Aphrodite. Travis hears water run, giggles, and then "Yes." comes through the door. The lock clicks and the door slowly opens. Aphrodite walks back toward the enormous tub, her flimsy gown slides to the floor, exposing her full-length back, as she steps into the billowing bubbles. "Come in Travis. The water feels wonderful, and the bubbles tickle. Come in. You'll enjoy it," Travis feels he has lost control over his body as he slowly walks towards the frothy water.

Nicole is building courage to remove her clothes and take a shower. Two way mirrors, secret passageways, and peep holes in hanging portraits cloud her mind. *Damn, Travis should have paid more attention to me this evening. I'm going to have to find a way to get Aphrodite out of my game plan. I should go to his room and make sure he is not thinking about her. I should really go now.* Getting up, she opens her door and crosses the hallway to his door.

Opening his door, she sees Travis standing in the bathroom doorway, looking down at Aphrodite taking a bubble bath. One leg is extended up, out of the water. "Travis, can you see what that is on my toe? Could you be a sweetheart and wipe it off for me, please?" she coos.

Nicole screams "Travis, what the hell are you doing?"

Aphrodite looks over to Nicole with anger flashing in her squinted eyes, "you can leave now Nicole. You're not needed and do not belong here."

Travis has a glazed look in his eyes and is breathing heavy as he turns to looks at Nicole. Nicole runs toward Travis, pulls him out of the bathroom doorway, and then pushes him down onto his bed. Aphrodite is lifting herself out of the water when Nicole returns to slam the bathroom door shut. Nicole could not help but notice Aphrodite's youthful and trim body. "Travis, what were you just doing? You heard Merlin. Stay away from her."

"I don't know what happened. She ran into my room and into the bathroom before I knew what was happening."

Aphrodite opens the door wearing a short, very short, white terrycloth bathrobe. She carried the skimpy and lacey nightclothes across her arm. Strutting across the room, she gives Nicole a malicious smile. "I'll be back when unwanted company is gone." She exits backwards, blowing a kiss to Travis as she slowly closes the door.

Nicole hears Merlin scolding Aphrodite in the hallway. Staring at Travis with a contorted face, she said, "You know she is over three thousand years old. What's it like watching a mummy take a bath?"

Austin sits cross-legged on Dyllan's bed. "Man I could really learn to love living like this. How come your room is nicer than mine? I think I'll stay here tonight. Just to protect you from the boogey man. A person could have some bad nightmares sleeping in a scary old mansion like this."

"Yah, sure, you just have my comfort and secure sleep in mind. Well I don't think so. I'm perfectly capable of taking care of myself. The only thing scary in this place is you. I know what you want. You're not going to embarrass me in front of all these people. I have your number, and it's not protecting the damsel in distress," said Dyllan.

"But..."

"No buts. Now get out of here and go back to your room, before we find out there's a bed check. We'll get together tomorrow, after we find a little more of what's going on around here."

"O.K." Austin goes to his room. Opening his door, he finds the room dark. *Strange*, he thinks, *I'm sure I left the light on.* While fumbling around on the wall to find the switch, a bed stand light comes on.

The server from dinner, that Austin was trying to flirt with, is in his bed, a sheet pulled to her chin. A nervous smile on her face, "I'm tired of Aphrodite getting all the attention. She is no better looking than me, and she has a bad reputation. I don't enjoy walking around like a zombie manikin. I want to have fun too." Patting the mattress she says. "Now, come to bed."

Austin wakes at 4 A.M. and thinks out loud. *"And Merlin says you're not fully functional. Little does he know."* Exhausted, he falls back to sleep.

Austin stretched and rubs sleep from his eyes. It's a great morning. Rolling over to kiss his new found love; he gags, leans over the edge of the bed, and voids his stomach. Stretched out alongside him is a limp, wrinkled, pile of decayed matter that looks like a three-year-old corpse in a plastic blow up doll. Austin shakily gets out of bed, slipping in the muck he just hurled, and runs out of the door into Travis's room.

## Chapter 11

"She's dead Travis, she's dead. Help me. Oh my God, she's dead," shouts Austin. Travis is finally in a deep sleep, after rolling and tossing all night, dreaming of Aphrodite. Nicole sits up, covering herself with a clutched sheet, her mouth open. Travis forces his eyes open, the pumping adrenaline shocking his mind and nerves into action. He leaps out of bed.

"What the hell is the matter Austin?" he asks.

"She's dead, Travis, she's dead. Come on, you have to help me."

"I'm coming, let me get my pants on."

Nicole slides further under the sheet shrieking, "Austin, get out of here."

He looks confused, turns, and runs back across the hall into his room. The bag of matter is slowly disintegrating down into nothing.

Travis slides to a stop, looking down into the bed. "Oh crap! What is that?"

"That was the server I was talking to at dinner. Merlin said she was only functional as a server. I found her in my bed last night after Dyllan kicked me out of her room. Now what should I do? What will Merlin do? What the hell is going on around here?

Dyllan walks into Austin's room. "Austin, what did you do in your bed? That is nothing but disgusting. Nothing you ate at dinner last night even remotely resembles that pile of whatever in your bed."

Austin, thinking fast, did not want Dyllan to know what he and the server did last night. "I don't know, I woke up this morning and found this mess in bed with me."

Nicole walks into Austin's room and seeing Dyllan, did not want her to know she spent the night in Travis's room, protecting him from Aphrodite. "What's all the yelling about? Oh my god Austin, what is that in your bed? It almost looks like a blow up doll full of rotted garbage. What did you do last night?"

Merlin enters the room with Aphrodite on his arm. "Has anyone seen server 13? She did not report for work this morning, nor was she seen anytime during the night in her rest station." said Merlin.

Aphrodite looks up with an innocent expression. "Why I think some one was trying to be active outside her parameters. I think that awful mess in your bed is server number 13."

"Austin, was 13 in you room with you last night?" asked Merlin.

Austin looks at Dyllan, back to Merlin and Aphrodite, and then with lowered head, softly said. "Yes, she was telling me her problems, being restricted to her duties and what she could not do. I was trying to comfort her."

Aphrodite smiled knowingly at Austin, taking in his nakedness, especially from the waist down. Merlin nods in agreement. "Yes, Austin, I know you are telling the truth. Security cameras verify your story. Truth is a trait on which I place high esteem. Breakfast is being prepared. It will be ready shortly. Please come to the dining room when you are ready."

Merlin and Aphrodite leave the room walking to the staircase. "Come Aphrodite, we will get housekeeping up here to make everything clean and orderly."

"But, but, Merlin. We cannot allow…"

"Now Aphrodite, do not question my decision. Come we have work to do. You must prepare the way for Athena's arrival."

Charles Schwend

"Athena will not want Aphrodite in her company. She will not want another to distract from her beauty. I do not believe Athena will be comfortable here. She belongs with her olive trees that she created and the weaving students she taught. My virtues would overshadow hers. She would not find a man's eyes to caress her while I am here. We should consider someone else to bring over," she said.

Merlin, with a smile, studies her face. "Aphrodite, would Athena's presence threaten you?"

"Of course not, I am only thinking of Athena's fragile self image. I would not want to put her under any stress after her first materialization. You, if anyone, should know how stressful the first creation is. I would not want her returned because of incompatibility."

"Yes Aphrodite, I am sure of your good intentions, but we must continue our work. We must complete our mission. The time for the gathering of the Gods is coming. Come, we must start our preparations. The chosen four are almost ready."

Aphrodite muffles an uncontrolled laugh with her hand, "Yes, almost ready."

## Chapter 12

Merlin turns dials, setting multiple numbers on the array of panel buttons, monitoring the bank of digital readouts and sine waves on oscilloscope displays. Aphrodite watches with a learning eye as Merlin slowly pushes the review button. A turbulent mist forms in an upright tube. Miniature lightning crackles and pops through the cloudy mass. A nude female figure slowly forms and rotates in the ten-foot materialization chamber. "She is done," acknowledges Merlin with a smile.

Aphrodite frowns, her eyes showing anger. "She will not like this body. It is too... too...sensuous. She will not want the kind of attention this body will burden her with. She will not be able to cope with the demands of..."

Merlin glances at Aphrodite from the corner of his eye, knowing the real reasons behind the objections. He raises his left hand to stop her vocal concerns, simultaneously pushing the finalize button. Turning his attention to the horizontal chamber of life, he monitors a count down display on the base. He engages a switch and then adjusts a sliding lever to a pre-determined position. A jagged leap of electricity arcs through the chamber. On a sparkling slab of white marble, Athena forms, as the image in the upright glass tube clears. A spray of liquid, a baptism of sorts, washes the figure of a white powder, draining into a canister below. A fan builds speed and the long blonde hair caresses her body as it dries in the artificial breeze.

Athena's chest heaves with her first breath. A light cough from the oxygen rich air and a soft flare of her nostrils shows life. Merlin admires his work and smiles as her head turns to look at him. The end cap slowly swings open with a soft hiss, like a blown kiss, from the escaping pressure, and the railed bed slowly slides out. She does not move until Merlin approaches and takes her hand, lifting her up to a sitting position. She studies Merlin, and then Aphrodite, smiles and stands wobbly on her feet. Merlin steadies her, and then, taking her other hand leads her down off the platform to the floor. "Do not speak. I am Merlin. This is Aphrodite. Do you know who you are?"

Athena nods her head yes; opens her mouth to speak. Merlin places his forefinger to her lips. She stills, running her tongue over her lips when Merlin removes his finger.

Merlin leads his new re-creation across the floor to a circle of full-length mirrors with a rotating base in the middle. He studies this new life with a critical eye, smiling with satisfaction. Athena smiles back at Merlin. A mischievous smile forms on her mouth as she parts her lips to speak, "Why am I here, and to whom do I owe my allegiance?"

"You are here because you are needed, and you owe allegiance only to me as your re-creator."

"What is this language I speak and how do I know it?"

"You have too many questions so early in your new life. All your answers will come in time." With a flourishing gesture of his hand toward the mirrors, Merlin says, "Now, see what I have done. After you have become familiar with your new body, you will dress, and then you will enjoy the first feast of your new life." Athena stares at herself in the mirrors, smiling in appreciation of her reflection.

Merlin leaves the game room and Aphrodite approaches Athena. "When you are done admiring yourself, we had better cover you."

"But what is wrong with me like this? Why must I cover myself?"

"Because that is what we do in this time. Now hurry. There is clothing there. Get dressed. We must not keep Merlin waiting."

"Is clothing like yours there for me?"

"No you must wear what is right for you. You would not be correctly dressed in my clothing. Please select from what I have put out for you, then, after we eat, I will take you for a walk, to show you what is here. I will wait for you."

Aphrodite enters the circle of mirrors, admiring herself from 360-degree angles. Athena walks to the rack of clothes on the opposite side of the room. Aphrodite is smoothing her short and revealing gown, emphasizing her body features when Athena calls to her.

"Aphrodite, come and help me select something to wear. I believe your opinion is important and needed, so I may suitably present myself."

"Just pick out anything. It is all suitable for you," replied Aphrodite. A tearing of cloth draws Aphrodite's attention from herself. Looking back at Athena, she sees her modifying the length and fit of a toga like gown. Athena slips on the now, low cut, short piece of cloth that hugs her breast, waist and hips and accentuating her long shapely legs.

"Aphrodite, will this do?"

"Yes," Aphrodite swears in disgust.

"Aphrodite, what will I put on my feet? Surely I am not expected to go without footwear?"

Aphrodite smiles. "Look on the shelving under the counter. There are sandals that will fit you perfectly." *Yes, ugly flip-flops that will be perfect for you, you old cow.* Aphrodite could not help but chuckle at her coup in exchanging the rubber monstrosities for the high fashion laced gladiator shoes originally there. Aphrodite looks back as Athena tears out the rubber loops, slips silk ribbon through the holes and up her calves. *I will get rid of her yet*, promises Aphrodite.

Escorting Athena to the dining room, Aphrodite wishes for Athena to trip, walk into statues or crash into floor vases. Nothing happens. Athena is much too graceful to experience mishap.

"Ah, here she is," exclaimed Merlin. "Aphrodite, sit Athena at the place of honor, the head of the table opposite me."

Aphrodite's face flushes with anger. "But, that is where I sit."

Merlin studies Aphrodite. "You can sit here beside me."

The four gawking guests enter the dinning room as Athena is seated. "Ah, perfect timing. Be seated and breakfast will be served." Nodding his head, Merlin commands, "Serve breakfast." Fruits, cereals, drinks, toast and spreads are place on the table. Everything is at the peak of their life and preparation. Athena sampled sparingly while studying the four young guests. Travis especially took her interest.

Aphrodite, noticing Athena's interest in Travis, glowers at her. "Athena, you were the favorite of Zeus and yet you allowed the Greeks to plunder Cassandra while she was under your protection. Why is that?"

Athena's eyes chilled. "The heat of battle from the Trojan War has long cooled. Its muck should not be dredged up from where it belongs. History died in the past, not to be resurrected in the present."

Merlin, eager to prevent conflict said, "War is not a suitable topic for a breakfast. I think our young guests would enjoy a lighter subject. Their enlightenment of the day would be better received. Nicole, what creation would you like to try today, clothes or maybe a vase?"

"Adonis, yes Adonis would be nice."

Aphrodite moans, "Merlin, you couldn't bring Adonis. You know our history. He cannot be here and not in my presence. He cannot be with me and not with me. My presence would tear him asunder."

Nicole smiles; *At last I have the ammunition to fight that ancient relic from the past.*

Merlin hesitates. "I think we can accommodate Adonis and his problems. Aphrodite, you know he would have to come eventually. You must prepare yourself, to ready yourself and make remedial plans to mentor his evolution into a contributing member of our group.

Aphrodite cannot control the anguish on her face. She knows having Adonis is impossible and also knows that seeing him, and touching him, would shatter the essence of them both. She lowers her head in submission to Merlin's wishes, as a tear rolls down her cheek, onto her hand. A thought blooms in her mind. *I wish I were never re-created by Merlin.*

After breakfast, Merlin takes Nicole into the game room. There he shows her how to program the equipment. Nicole watches Merlin intensely, asking questions as Merlin looks up the physical and mental definitions of Adonis.

"You know of course, that this creation will not be good for Aphrodite at this time."

Nicole looks into Merlin's eyes thoughtfully. "Yes, but it will keep her occupied, and her thoughts off my friends and I."

"Very good, then let us begin. Review these traits that are inherent to Adonis. If you wish to deviate from the norm of his characteristics we will see a report on this screen, listing any repercussions or conflicts the deviation will cause. This will aid you in your final decision."

"No, I feel we should keep his original psyche intact, but can we remove any influential connection with Aphrodite and Persephone?"

Pleasure fills Merlin's face. "Yes, a good decision. We will have to make an adjustment here, to his more youthful time, keeping in mind that his mental and physical capacities were not yet fully developed, and we will also have to build in a mental resistance to their attraction. Yes, this will be interesting to see." Merlin concentrates on a monitor. "Here comes the report on your choices of change. Yes, his mental make up is indeed more stable, but a little more independent." With final adjustments made, Merlin walks Nicole through the remaining process.

As the end cap of the horizontal chamber of life hisses open, Adonis slides out for examination. Nicole's eyes dilate, nostrils flare and her breathing becomes heavy as Merlin helps Adonis to stand. He stares at Nicole and her knees feel like they are made of jello wanting to buckle. She feels emotions she has never experienced before.

With a trembling finger she wipes tears from her cheeks, murmuring, "Oh god, I don't believe this. He is the most beautiful thing I have ever seen." She quickly steps back, unsteadily, to sit on a chair.

Merlin, pleased with the re-creation, leads Adonis to the circle of mirrors. "Look at yourself Adonis." Adonis slowly rotates before the mirrors, looking at himself from all angles, a smile filling his face. Merlin enjoys the expression on his face. "Adonis, speak to me. What do you think?"

"What is that reflective surface? Is it magic? Are you a magician?"

"Adonis this is called a mirror. No, it is not magic, and yes, I am a magician. I am the most accomplished magician the world has ever known. And now, with what I can do, I will be known until the end of time. Now tell me what do you think of yourself? Are you pleased with what you see?"

"Yes, I am pleased. Thank you for what you have done"

Merlin steps back and motions toward Nicole. "Adonis, Nicole is your designer. You should thank Nicole for all that you see and feel."

Nicole flushes as Adonis turns to stare at her. His smile brings flutters to her stomach, and she cannot break away from their locked eyes. *Oh my god, I can't trust myself around him. Why did I do this?* Nicole's eyes gaze at his hair, taking in the chiseled facial features then dropping to his neck and broad muscular shoulders. His chest is wide and thick, tapering down to a slim waist and narrow hips. Her eyes linger on the hip and upper thigh area. Her breath catching until she forces herself to drop her focus down to the well toned calves then beautiful turned ankles and feet.

Nicole knows she cannot let Merlin and Adonis know her thoughts; she stands and hastily leaves the room to rejoin the others. She finds them in the library with Aphrodite and Athena. Aphrodite is reclining on the Greek reclined bench. With lowered eyes Aphrodite watches Athena playing a harp and sing. The descriptive musical love lyrics do not help Nicole's fluttering stomach or shaky nerves. Taking a couple of deep breaths, she pours herself a glass of lemonade from a serving tray, wishing for something stronger. Dyllan studies Nicole before coming over to her. "Nicole, is something wrong? You look flushed." Noticing the shaking glass in her hand, she asks, "What's wrong? I've never seen you like this."

"You would look like this too. You would not believe what I just went through."

Merlin and Adonis enter the library. "There you are Nicole, why did you leave so suddenly?" Receiving no answer, Merlin looks at the group. "Everyone, this is Adonis. What do you think?" Adonis is clothed in modern clothes, shorts, polo sweater, and sandals that emphasized his athletic build and looking like he was ready for a game of tennis.

Aphrodite wet her lips with the tip of her tongue. Athena set down the harp, then seductively walks over to Adonis as if for a closer examination. When face to face, Athena brushes Adonis' cheek with the back of her hand, quietly moaning "Hhhmmmmm", and then returns to her harp with a sad expression on her face. Adonis did not smile but has a perplexed look on his face. Merlin gazed over the gathering then said to Adonis, "Come with me. We will get some nourishment in you." Then Merlin escorts Adonis toward the dining room.

## Chapter 13

"Adonis, who would you wish to bring over next?" asked Merlin.

"Some one who will bring peace to the group," exclaimed Adonis. "I feel tension and competition between the female gods. I think we need one who would not hesitate to place themselves in harms way to protect the whole. One who would not challenge or provoke, but rather calm and rationalize with example. I think Artemis would bring out the better attributes of Aphrodite and Athena, and show the merits of non-competitive beauty. Yes definitely Artemis."

"A very good selection Adonis," said Merlin. "After sating your appetite, you will be apprised of your role in Merlin's house, and what is expected of you. Then a walk through what is here, before we welcome Artemis to our gathering. Yes, a very excellent choice.

Artemis will indeed be a neutralizing buffer between Aphrodite and Athena," *and yourself.* "Now, what food would you like? Before entering the dining room, let me warn you of the hazards of you charming the female servers who attend to the needs of this house," said a smiling Merlin.

Adonis stops and looked at Merlin. "Are all the women of the house as beautiful as Aphrodite and Athena? How is a male able to survive their charm and beguilement?"

Merlin answers with a serious tone, "Godly control Adonis, Godly control."

Adonis studies the women servers as he consumes his food. Several times he stops and looks at Merlin as though he might ask a question to which he received a slow side-to-side movement of Merlin's head. Adonis decides to keep his questions in reserve until a more appropriate private interlude presents itself. He did continue to enjoy the beauty of the servers that appear equal to Aphrodite and Athena, while their communicative skills lack in depth and content. He noticed that Merlin controlled the activities of the dining room attendants with eye movements, head nods and other body language. He is definitely the maestro of this culinary orchestration.

Taking his lead from Merlin, Adonis finished his meal, placing utensils and napkin on his dinnerware. Raising his wine goblet in a salute, Merlin said. "Finish your wine and we will go to the game room and explore what values to give Artemis."

"Yes, I would enjoy that," replied Adonis. "I would like her to be compatible to my needs, and fulfill herself by being my companion."

Merlin frowns. *Did I miscalculate the building blocks creating the matrix of Adonis? I will have to be more deliberate and cautious in future designing.*

Merlin gestures, getting up to leave, with Adonis following. Merlin enters the game room and starts entering the formulation data into the matrix of life to re-create Artemis.

"Will she bring her bow and arrows, nymphs and dogs?" asked Adonis.

"No." replied Merlin. "But she will bring her hunting skills, keeping the nights from darkness with the moon's bright light, while running unclothed through the woods, cavorting with the wild deer. She is one of the more complex Gods, being both good and bad. Therefore, I will enhance the good and diminish the bad attributes to make her a more effective member of our group and in tune with our goals."

"And what are our goals, Merlin?"

"We will change the world into a place of love and harmony. We will eliminate war and despair. We will create a paradise for all, and we will be like Gods, enjoying the fruits of our labors. We will lead by example and teach with guidance."

Merlin keyed in data, referencing his old hand scribed book, detailing physical description and mental properties listed under Artemis. "Should I change anything?" Merlin mutters out loud to himself.

Adonis thinking that Merlin was asking him nearly shouted out his reply, "No, she must be exactly the same. She must look as she was."

Merlin presses the review button and a nude female body forms in the swirling mist of the glass materialization chamber. Crackling lightning momentarily makes shadowy features of the re-creation visible to Adonis. The mist starts to clear revealing an upright goddess slowly rotating. A tear slides down and off the cheek of Adonis. "She is the most beautiful of all."

Merlin turns his head toward Adonis as he pushes the finalize button. "Is she more beautiful then Athena or even Aphrodite?"

Adonis waits to answer as his attention is drawn to the horizontal chamber of life where a figure forms, while the body in the materialization chamber dissolves.

"Yes, more beautiful. She is perfection. I will have to protect her from the others who will feel her presence as a threat. I will have to be her constant companion."

Once again, the chamber of life gives birth to an ancient God. Merlin stands back as Adonis smothers Artemis with attention, grooming her for introduction and preening her to his own satisfaction. Artemis shows resistance to the hovering, trying to distance herself, first with looks, then outstretch arm and finally with voice. "Have you no respect. Leave me until I am presentable. I am not a piece of ripe fruit to be devoured. Let me breathe." Looking at Merlin she says. "Where am I? Why am I here? Why would you have me unclothed, vulnerable to those with less than honorable intent? Do you not realize who I am?"

Merlin, with the polish from successfully dealing with kings and their courts said, "Artemis, the Goddess of the hunt, deer, wood nymphs, and the matriarch of archery, has been called to this time, to lead the Gods in the world's quest. You are asked to be the pivotal link, the interpreter of the Gods and of mankind. You were selected because of your legend and prowess. You alone are capable to accomplish what must be done."

Artemis, with a smile of acknowledgement, replied, "Why have I not been suitably dressed or made presentable? Why am I chilled with no robe or covering?

Who are you, one too old to warm me, and the other too young to know how?"

Adonis, reprimanded, retreats to stand beside Merlin, looking dejected and insulted. Merlin, knowing Artemis's psyche, smiled knowingly. "I could only bring your body to this time, but I have prepared for your arrival with dress and accessories that are to your liking. Come, first we must clothe you, and then equip you with weapons of which you will marvel. Come now, so we may enhance your beauty." Merlin stretches out his hand, indicating the wardrobe and rack of accessories.

Artemis ignores the eye contact from Adonis, focusing instead on the togas, dresses, shoes and combs. Holding up a bra and panties, she asked, "What manner of clothing are these?"

"Those are underclothing. In your right hand is a bra to be used for supporting your breasts and in your left hand are panties to be used as under garments. They are used by all women in this time for many good reasons," said Merlin.

"I will wear this, what you call a bra, but I have no use for this thin, small piece of clothing. I do not see what good it would do for me."

Merlin chuckled, "I would recommend you try wearing the panties. I believe you will find it quite comfortable. If you don't like it, you can always remove it."

Artemis looked up at Merlin as she was lifting her leg to put on the panties. Noticing his intense stare, she rotated her body to afford him only a side view to allow her a little privacy.

She feels a lack of respect for a Goddess of her stature. She stares at the bra before realizing its intended use, and then deftly secures it at her back with hooks. She selects a pair of silk walking shorts and a fitted opened neck, button down blouse. *These should be comfortable and full enough for hunting.* She selects a pair of practical knee length boots with low heels to complete her attire. Merlin indicates the mirrors and revolving platform with a hand gesture. Stepping on the platform, her eyes crinkle in pleasant surprise at her appearance and a smile of satisfaction graces her mouth. Adonis moans.

Stepping away from the mirrors, Artemis sees a compound bow with a quiver of nicely fletched arrows. Her excitement and pleasure shows while handling and admiring the weapon. She delicately knocks an arrow, placing the notch of the arrow onto the bowstring then slowly turned, sighting around the room, stopping at Adonis who shows a look of disbelief. A smile of malevolence twists her mouth into a sinister sneer. "Do you still feel I would be a suitable one to cower before your attempt of control and dominance?"

Adonis stutters, "No, no. I was only... I am... I need... I have been in awe of you forever. I am the reason you are here. You were selected by me to come to this time for the reasons Merlin told you. I have nothing but love and respect for you. I..."

Artemis left fly the arrow notched on her string, narrowly missing Adonis' ear and imbedding itself into the wall. "This weapon is very accurate." She smiled. *Yes, this should keep him at a proper distance until I learn what is needed in this strange place of questionable men.* "Can I keep this bow and quiver of arrows?"

"Yes," replied Merlin, "but the weapon should be kept here and not carried around the dwelling. Others may be fearful of its possible misuse."

## Chapter 14

Professor Mundez sits at his newly acquired Redwood desk with his back to the windows and their view of the duck pond under a bright moonlight. *Now that I have taken over the science department, I'll make everyone follow my revolutionary, cutting edge thinking. This university will be the leading educational science facility in the nation. M.I.T. – look out.*

A cool gentle breeze gently wafts the back of his neck. A cold chill runs down his spine and a shiver courses through his body. *Now What?* He turns his head to check if the windows might be open. Getting up, he walks into the adjoining room, his outer office, to check the windows there. All the windows are closed. Returning to his inner office he stops in the doorway, unable to understand what he is seeing. He grabs the doorknob to keep from falling. A heavy sweat soaks his clothes. Every breath is a pain as he forces himself to breath. He does not know if he is having a heart attack, or, is experiencing a hallucination that one has before passing out.

Sitting in his chair is Professor Ambrose Hamlock, smiling at him, legs crossed and his elbow resting on the desk. "Professor Jago Mundez. How wonderful to see you again. I have found a rare exotic tea that you would just die to taste. Come and sit down. I have prepared it just the way you like. It is extremely stimulating. It will make you feel untamed and wild, like a young horse. Come sit. I have missed our little chats and have been looking forward to you joining me."

Mundez clutches his chest. Pain radiates down his left arm. His chest seizes, as his heart feels squeezed. His breath would not come. The vise grip on the doorknob relaxes and let go, as he slowly crumples to the floor. His fixed eyes stare at Hamlock taking a sip of cool water from the teacup he had just offered.

Wiping everything he touched, Hamlock, leaving the teacup half filled with cool water, departs by the back office door. *You win some and you lose some. I guess Jago lost this one. I hope someone finds him before he smells up my office.*

Merlin opens the driver's door for him. "You know I could have dispatched him more easily, in a more creative manner, than that clumsy feat."

"Yes, but doing it my way gave me a tremendous sense of satisfaction, and it was clean, fast and very humane. The unknowing world is better off, now that he is gone."

"I should drive back to the house. I need the practice before taking my driver's test. You said that I would need my license to be mobile in this time."

"Yes, you should not have to rely on others for transportation. Are you sure you're ready for this? You have never driven at night. It could be tricky with the bright oncoming lights, and your vision diminished in the dark of night."

"I believe that I am capable of driving back. I have been watching the moving images you provided and cannot foresee any difficulties."

"Yes, like trying to learn how to swim by watching instructional videos. All right, here, take the keys. Remember, I'll be watching you like a hawk. You make one big mistake and you're out of the driver's seat."

"Does everyone go through this humiliating process in this time?"

"Only if they want to drive, now quit complaining and take me home."

Arriving home, Merlin parks in a monstrous garage, enters by the front door, announcing his arrival by shouting, "I am back and need a refreshing drink, a cool glass of ale."

Ambrose walks to the side of the house hidden by thick shrubbery and silently enters through a secret entrance, invisible to a casual eye. Silently walking down padded steps, he enters a secluded part of the basement that has access to a lower, sub-basement level, serving as his temporary living quarters.

Cassidy, his personal assistant is waiting with his favorite drink, sassafras cordial. Cassidy, or Cass as he nicknamed her, is the most intelligent of all his re-creations. He used the beauty of Aphrodite, the wisdom of Merlin, the cunning of Mercury, and the practicality of Hesiod to mold her mind, self-image and beauty. When Merlin becomes an equal, a partner in his endeavors, Cass will be second in the hierarchy.

Up 'til now, he had always wondered if all the hidden passageways and doors were really necessary. His attention to future, *what if,* scenarios resulted in the perfect solution to his re-created presence. Here he made plans, free from distraction. Here he could focus on the future and it's priorities.

The necessary activity of the evening is dismissed from his mind as more pressing issues need to be resolved. He called for Cass to sit and contribute to his train of thoughts.

"Cass, I did something terrible tonight. I killed Professor Mundez. There was no way for me to control him. He had an insane drive to become head of the science department. If he had waited until I retired, my position would have been his. He was in an awful hurry, and once at my desk he would have hung on like a wolverine. What do you think, Cass, did I do the right thing? I feel terrible about it."

"I am sure you did what you had to do. I also feel he would have had a negative effect on your current plans. I would have feared for the safety of your niece, Nicole. Yes, you took the right action. If in the future, you are in a position to contain Professor Mundez's violent tendencies and malevolent thinking, a re-creation might be appropriate."

"Cass, you do have a way to simplify the most complex issues. You have been a great help in easing my conscience. I feel sleep will be easier for me tonight because of your settling reassurance. Thank you my dear. Please bring another bottle of my cordial, maybe black raspberry, and then, why don't you retire for the night. Anything not finished can wait until morning.

There will be nothing more you can do for me until then."

After the cordial was placed on the end table, Cassidy left through a hidden door. Professor Hamlock could smell her lingering perfume. Thoughts of her and the glass of cordial relaxed him and planning for the future consumed his mind. Plans must be meticulously made. *There can be no complications causing deviation. There must be a complete fruition. What would I do without Cass and Merlin?*

**Chapter 15**

Monday morning starts with a gentle knock. A server enters to set the table for breakfast, leaves and then returns with a tray of food. Ambrose watches her with deep satisfaction. *She is beautiful and intelligent, but somewhat limited in function. A more perfect being would be impossible to accomplish. How could anyone want anything more? Merlin is an astute pupil. Soon he will be an equal in our endeavor to make a better world.*

The smell of breakfast breaks his train of thought. The food and morning tea soon puts him into a trance like state. Pleasure fills his mind and stirs his body. His thoughts go back to the server. *Why you old fool, you are an academic and too old to be having youthful thoughts like that, or, are you never too old to think?* A smile graced his face as his thoughts deepen. *If only I were younger and knew what I know now.*

Merlin enters the room. "Professor, I would like to begin making preparations for your niece, Nicole, and her companions to take more responsibilities in accomplishing our plans... What are you thinking about? I have never seen that expression on you before. If I did not know better..."

"Yes Merlin, I was thinking the very same thing. They need suggestive conditioning to bring them more in line with our objectives. Who do you believe would be the best to accomplish this?"

"Not Aphrodite. Not Athena and definitely not Adonis. They would become suspicious of you and I. Artemis ...Artemis would be best received by the four. She would be more readily identified as one of them. She is the most practical of all the Gods, but she too, would need a period of indoctrination in order to smoothly meld our goals with their beliefs."

"Yes, I agree. Artemis is out hunting, for what I do not know, but she finds her solace in the wilderness, cavorting with who knows what. She is more perceptive than I realized. Adonis can attest to that. Has he recovered yet?"

Merlin chuckles, "She put a real scare in him. He is very quiet and withdrawn when she is present, especially when she is carrying her weapon. He leaves when she gives him that look. I never knew she was so assertive and dominating. I am hoping she will start mingling with the others as she gets more acquainted with them.

She will be included in more activities with the group. Aphrodite and Athena will not stay in the same room alone with her. They are still just a little cautious. There must be something more in her past than either of us knew. There is still time."

Merlin studied Ambrose then asked, "Professor, when will you let Nicole and her three friends know that you are alive and well?"

"Soon, Merlin, soon, she must be ready, and accepting of our plans for the future. I do not think she is thinking conceptually of what we do and my being alive. She just now understands how my recent death has affected her life. I plan on her taking charge of that youthful group. They will carry on my work when we are fulfilling our own ambitions. What we must do now is to think of a process to bring our gods together into a cohesive group. They must learn to act as one, not like a drop of water that splatters in all directions when confronting a test of their unified will. Now, Merlin, would you like to join me for breakfast?"

"No. I have duties elsewhere. The servers are complaining that Number 13 must be replaced. Her duties assumed by the others are becoming a burden to them. I believe re-creating Number 13 would be my best option. If I re-created another original server they would feel replaceable with little self worth. But, if I re-create Number 13 everything will be as it was, with all retaining a sense of worth. I feel that running the large staff required in this place of interwoven whirlwinds, that pulls me in all directions, is the most demanding position that has ever befallen me."

"Merlin, actions only speak of your skill, knowledge and endurance. You are more than my right hand. You are my equal. Without you, I would not be. Your words are honored before my own. Do not speak lightly of yourself before me. Now, do what you must, but keep me advised."

**Chapter 16**

The mid-morning sun brightens the library. From opposite ends of the long table, Aphrodite and Athena were eyeing each other with suspicion, eating a breakfast pastry. Aphrodite stops mid bite, keeping her gaze locked on Athena, waiting for eye contact. When Athena's eyes rose to hers, Aphrodite said, "We must join together and put aside our petty jealousies and suspicions. Only through cooperation will we be strong enough to enjoy ourselves in this new life of ours. Our liaison will need to be kept secret to avoid possible reprisal from the others."

"Yes, how remarkable; I was also having the same thoughts. We need to put our differences away until we find what roads we each must take. We now have fortunes not available in our former existence. We can become normal immortal humans. Not Gods of stories, statues or paintings. We can now feel true emotion. Our lives will be believable. We can achieve what we want, by ourselves. We can be... be...legendary, not myth or fiction."

"We must be careful. If the servant staff finds us out, they will tell Merlin. He would not feel kindly toward our desires. The professor and he have plans for us, and I am sure we will not like their plans. We have both been abused in our prior life, submissive in our actions and reasoning. Yes, we will have to be very careful."

"Aphrodite, what life would you most like?"

"A normal human family, with immortality, without the glitz and glamour that follow us like jokers and their musical entourage. I so tire of the attention and fixation it draws. I would like a loving spouse, and children that could be gathered around, and watch them grow to adulthood. Yes, counseling the children, nurturing them until they are tall, strong and wise. Yes, a family of normal humans."

"Could Artemis be trusted with our alliance? Could she possibly join us? If so, we three would be stronger than just two. How can we know if she can be trusted? She feels more for her dogs and deer than anyone or anything else. She must be approached very carefully to avoid revealing our pact."

**Chapter 17**

Nicole motions to Dyllan, with a nod of her head, toward the French doors leading out to a small garden. Dyllan pans the library to see if anyone was watching, and then follows Nicole outside. Sitting next to Nicole on a wooden bench she said, "O.K. Nicole, what's going on? You're as nervous as mouse in a snake pit."

"I've been watching Aphrodite and Athena. There is something going on between them, and their expressions are different now; there is no animosity or jealousy like before. They were always arch enemies and now they are acting like best friends."

"You're right Nicole, I caught them whispering to each other when they thought no one was watching. They had better not be plotting to get Austin or Travis. I don't care if they do call themselves Gods, I'll take them down, or, at least tell Merlin. I know he will do something about it."

"Well whatever they're up to, you know it's no good. Before we just had to worry about Aphrodite and now with Athena to watch it will be a lot harder. Austin and Travis won't have a chance against them unless we keep on our toes."

"We should check out that old book that Merlin keeps in his so called game room. There just might be something in there that could be useful to us. You know, like a magic potion, or spell or something. Nicole, we need to sneak in there tonight after everyone goes to sleep. I guess they sleep, don't they?"

"I don't know, but whatever we do, we had better not alienate Merlin. He has stood up for us so far."

*Yes, we cannot make Merlin mad, at least not until Uncle Hamlock's estate is through probate,* thought Dyllan. "Nicole, just act natural when we go back in. We just came out for some fresh air and to look at the garden plants."

The flow of fresh air in the room caught the attention of everyone in the library as they watched Dyllan and Nicole enter and close the door. The more they tried to act casual the more their actions drew notice. Nicole's eyes passed from person to person, until she sat down with her back to the room.

Dyllan was forced to sit opposite of Nicole, a focal point for the staring group.

"Oh thanks a lot Nicole. I can't even scratch my nose with everyone looking, waiting for me to do something. Why didn't you sit here?"

"Just relax Dyllan. Act normal. No don't act normal. That would just make them suspicious. Act like me, relaxed, like nothing is going on. Come on, just think of all that nervousness dropping down and flowing out your toes, out onto the floor, where those two, Aphrodite and Athena could slip in it and fall on their rears. Now that would relax everyone. Really give them all a laugh. Come on, smile, and laugh a little."

"Right, just laugh for no reason. That will make me look innocent and give me something to laugh about."

"Do what they tell speakers to do. Imagine that they are all in their underwear, or naked. No, don't do that. That won't make you laugh. I forgot about Adonis, I have to keep you calm. Better yet, imagine all the women with beards and the men with lipstick. That should bring on a smile or two."

Dyllan broke out in a big smile and started a loud boisterous laugh, which made everyone stop and stare. Then they also started to laugh.

"What's so funny Dyllan?" questioned Artemis.

"Yah, tell us the joke," said Travis.

## Chapter 18

One a.m. and the house is finally quiet with the lights dimmed. Dyllan and Nicole creep down the grand staircase. Noises are heard from the kitchen. *I guess the kitchen staff does not all retire for the night,* thought Dyllan. Putting a finger to her pursed lips to indicate silence, Dyllan led Nicole slowly down the steps. Reaching the massive door to the game room, Dyllan cautiously turns the doorknob, slowly pushing the door open. The hinges resist the movement. The screech sounds like cat claws on a chalkboard to Nicole, while in reality it is only a soft kitty creak. A dim night-light pushes soft shadows out from the equipment. Quiet humming is ominous in its monotone sound.

Searching for and finding the console desk, Dyllan and Nicole carefully make their way through the obstacles obstructing their path. Stools, chairs, a book and un-named tools carelessly strewn by the day's activities are evaded. The drawer holding Merlin's book appears to be locked, but after a little tugging comes loose from a binding twist.

"Oh my God, we forgot to bring a flashlight," whispered Dyllan.

"Wait. There is a small lamp here somewhere. Let me find it. It's right... dammit".

"What's the matter? What happened?" asked Dyllan.

"One of those damned gods left an open brooch on the counter top, and of course I just happened to find it. Here's the lamp. There." A light floods the area. A towel draped over the back and sides of the lampshade cut back the light flooding the room. The book is heavy and lands with a thump. Eagerness surpasses caution as ancient paper rips from the rapid page turning.

"I don't understand what's written here. It's sure not English, or English I know. When the hell was this book written?" asks Dyllan.

"Let me try it."

"Knock your brains out. If you can understand that gibberish, you're a better person than me."

"Wait," said Nicole. "This book was written in Merlin's first lifetime. I really don't think they could understand themselves back then and..."

"We could understand each other and ourselves very well," said Merlin walking out of the darkness. "We had words that meant something, unlike that 'gibberish' used now. Cool; awesome; LOL; BFF, give me great stress and a pain in my head. People who talk like that also give me a pain in my lower region. Why are you destroying my ledger? What are you looking for?"

Dyllan and Nicole glance at each other. Nicole stammers but can not pronounce any words. Dyllan quickly recovers and said, "We were just trying to get better ideas on what to do with all this equipment. We really need to be able to catch up with the others. They seem so knowledgeable for just arriving in this time. And..."

"And, you thought a few appropriate spells would help you handle the Gods better," said Merlin. "You don't need my book for that. They are very vulnerable in this time and place. Give them good information on mingling, using thought and action with the people of this time, and you will not have to think of spells and schemes. I will forget this has happened. Come to me for advice, I know more about the Gods and how they think, than the Gods themselves. Now return to your quarters. You will need to be well rested for the coming day." Dyllan and Nicole leave as if to return to their bedrooms, and Merlin follows to consult with Professor Hamlock.

"I don't trust Merlin," said Nicole. "We should follow him and see what he's up to. Why should we trust him? He's in cahoots with the Gods."

"O.K., let's follow him. He's always just showing up, out of nowhere. He may be a magician, but I don't believe in magic. Yes, we should follow him and learn a few of his tricks. Take off your shoes. All the floors in this place are not carpeted and we don't want to be caught."

Dyllan and Nicole follow Merlin through the house, to the kitchen pantry and down a massive stone staircase to the basement. When they reach the basement floor, Merlin is gone, just disappeared. A dim light illuminates the basement allowing a canvassing of the area without knocking things over or making an alerting noise. While in the middle of the wine cellar they hear a door closing. Rushing to a corner reveals a door, leading to another stairway, carefully crafted to blend in with the wood covered walls. Putting their ears to the door, at the bottom of the stairs, they hear Merlin talking with someone.

Nicole knows the familiar sounding voice but cannot identify who it is. Suddenly Merlin said, "But Ambrose. They could be getting close to the truth."

*Ambrose! Merlin is talking to my uncle Hamlock. How can that be, he's dead*, thought Nicole. Dyllan has the same thought. They stare at each other with mouth open and eyes wide. Dyllan motions to Nicole to follow her and they retreat the way they came, back to Dyllan's bedroom. Not trusting that the room isn't bugged, Dyllan takes paper and pencil from her desk drawer and writes. "Don't talk. The room may be bugged. We'll write notes and take them to Austin and Travis, now."

Nicole carefully eases Travis's door open and enters a totally dark room. Feeling around the inside wall, she finds the switch and flips it on. The light temporarily blinds Nicole, and after a few seconds could see that Travis had his head under the covers. Quietly she crosses the room to the bed and gently eases the covers off a snoring Travis. Placing a cool hand on a hot shoulder produces a violent jerk and a loud scream of surprise.

"Sssshhh," shushed Nicole.

"What – What do you want? How did you know I was dreaming of you?" said Travis.

"Quiet, you'll wake the dead."

"Dead, whose dead? When?"

"No. Quiet down and look at this." Nicole shoves the note in front of Travis. *Professor Hamlock is alive and living in the basement.*

Travis's mouth opens to speak and Nicole barely covers it with her hand in time. She holds out her other index finger and shook her head from side to side, mouthing the word NO. Nicole mimes putting on a pair of pants and motions for Travis to follow her.

Dyllan cautiously looks up and down the corridor as she slowly backs up to Austin's door. Turning the knob, she pushes the door open with her rump. She winced when Austin's light cast her shadow back onto the floor. "Nitwit," she murmured. Austin was on his bed staring at her with anticipation, a large smile on his face. The television was on with the sound turned down. "What the hell are you watching?" Dyllan said.

Austin quickly grabs the remote and turns the TV off. "Nothing, I was just channel surfing."

Dyllan walked to the bed with a purpose. Austin thinks the purpose is to get in and he rolls over to make room for her. Again, that bigger than life smile, plays across his face.

Looking around Dyllan places her forefinger to her lips, and again Austin takes her actions for another meaning.

Dyllan gives Austin a look of disgust, motioning with her finger to come closer. When Austin comes over and sits at the edge of his bed, she slaps him on top of the head. Austin closes his eyes in reflex and when they open, Dyllan has a piece of paper in front of his face and again place her forefinger to her lips.

Austin starts to read aloud, "Pro…"

"Quiet you idiot, just read to yourself," she whispers.

Austin mouthed the words quietly to himself. *Professor Hamlock is alive and living in the basement.* An animation comes over Austin's face as he mouths more words, "What? Your nuts, there is no way."

Dyllan picks up and hands Austin's his pants, beckoning him to follow her. Austin's face changes from a state of heightened anticipation to an adventurous seriousness.

## Chapter 19

As pre-arranged, the four meet in the garden by the waterfall. Nicole and Dyllan stammer in excitement while Travis and Austin sit on the seat encircling the water staring at each other in bewilderment.

"Are you sure?" questioned Travis.

"Do you think I don't know my own uncle's voice?" said Nicole.

"I can't believe this. There has to be some mistake," said Austin.

"You know what I think, Merlin brought Uncle Ambrose back. That would explain everything. But why didn't he tell me. Surely he would trust me to know. Maybe I should go to him and ask for an explanation?" said Nicole.

"What makes you think your uncle would be up front with you now, when he wasn't before?" asked Travis.

"I feel he will be somewhat honest once he realizes we know he's alive," replied Nicole.

Austin looks at his friends and quietly said, "Nicole, you don't know who or what he has with him. I just don't know. You could be walking into a dangerous situation, if you confront him. I see all kind of new things, people that I haven't seen around before. And Merlin, I don't think we should trust him one bit. He's down right scary. You never know what is going to pop out of thin air when he's around."

"No, I'll be O.K. He's my uncle. I'll be perfectly safe with him. Remember, I will inherited everything he owned."

"Exactly, you will now legally own everything he had before his death. What makes you think he doesn't want everything back? I think we should sleep on this for tonight and get together tomorrow to make a decision. Maybe this would give Professor Hamlock time to come to you and volunteer the information," said Travis. Everyone nods heads in agreement.

"O.K., we'll get together after breakfast. We can meet back here and make a decision before Merlin decides to have us re-create someone, or something else.

We need to have a serious discussion before deciding on another re-creation," said Nicole.

"Back to bed everyone, and if you run into anyone, act natural. You were just out walking to get some fresh air," said Dyllan.

The four find no sleep. Restless and tossing the rest of the night, they are in a sleepless daze when knocks rap on their doors announcing breakfast. Quick showers and fresh clothes make them feel somewhat better. Walking down to the dining room together, they encounter the aromas of breakfast. "I'm going to be as fat as a pig if they keep serving that food. I'm addicted to it. Where do those recipes come from? I've never heard of most of it. People must have been really fat back when. I hope there is an English description after the menu items. I can't even pronounce most of those dishes. Merlin seems to take delight in keeping us confused and relying on him to explain everything to us," said Nicole.

Merlin was seated and drinking from a teacup as they entered. "You're awake and ready for a new day. How do they say it now? Bright eyed and bushy tailed. I think we..."

"I'm not very bright eyed and I know there is no bushy tail following me around," grimace Dyllan. "I think we just need breakfast and a short nap in the garden to soak up some sun."

Merlin studied the four for a moment, and then said, "I do not believe you will be soaking up any sun today. It's cloudy and misting. The weatherman said it would last all day."

"Good, then we will just soak up some rain," responded Dyllan.

Merlin again studied each of the four, and said nothing. Breakfast is ordered and placed before them by a crew of smiling and cheerful servers. Austin is so tired; he at first did not notice a twin to server number 13, place two twelve inch waffles with fresh strawberries and berry syrup down before him. A gentle nudge with her hip fails to draw his attention away from the bouquet rising from the delicacy in front of him. The four cannot curtail smiles of culinary satisfaction. A second serving is called upon before silverware could be rested on cleaned plates. A Mayan chocolate drink, sweetened with honey as clear as water, was served, as everyone savored a restful period following the waffles.

"Well, if anyone is interested, I have some intriguing duties to attend to," said Merlin.

"No thanks, we would not be very attentive companions this morning. I think we will try to catch up on our rest. We should be alert and more communicative this afternoon," replied Nicole.

"There is a canopy up in the courtyard and a server can attend to any needs you may have," said Merlin in a helpful voice.

Dyllan turns to look at Merlin. A forced smile is on her face. "Thank you. Some lounge chairs would also be nice, but I don't think we'll need a server. Thank you for your considerate thoughts."

## Chapter 20

Meeting in the garden, Nicole immediately takes charge stating, "I think I should search out my uncle and tell him we know what is happening. What do you think?"

Dyllan looks at her three companions before replying. "I think we should all approach your uncle. We would be a unified front. Your uncle would be less likely to try to intimidate us as a group. But first we have to find him. He may not be in that basement room now, where we heard him talking to Merlin."

Austin takes a half step closer and in a subdued voice said, "But that is the only reference point we have. We need to start there. We should be able to find someone there that knows where he's at."

The four retrace Nicole and Dyllan's path from the previous evening. Cautiously stepping close to the stairwell entrance, Nicole put her ear to the door. There is no sound. Slowly she turns the knob and eases the door open. There is no resistance or noise from the opening door. The light in the room is dim, but Professor Hamlock's head can be seen over the back of his chair. A lit floor lamp stands beside the chair.

"Merlin, I was not expecting you so early," said Hamlock.

"Uncle Ambrose, its Nicole. I need to talk to you."

Ambrose shot up from his chair, turning to look at Nicole and her three friends. "What are you doing here? How did you find me?"

"We followed Merlin last night and heard the two of you talking. Uncle Ambrose, why didn't you tell me you were back? Why did you keep everything a secret?"

Professor Hamlock's body sagged a little. He turned and sat back down. "Come over here and sit. I have a story to tell you." He waited until the four were seated, hesitating while he studied them.

"Well?" said Nicole.

"As you know, Professor Mundez murdered me, wanting to get his hands on all this," he said, waving his hands above his head. "Then he suffered a heart attack, with a little help from Merlin and I. We could not let anyone know that Merlin brought me back. How could I explain that without drawing international attention to what we are doing here?

"Merlin and I are putting together a group that will forever change the world to be a better place, a place of peace and harmony. Just think, no more wars, disease eradicated - a world of health, wealth and happiness."

"Oh yeah," exclaimed Nicole. "With Aphrodite in charge, I know what everyone would be doing. They would not have time or thought about health and wealth, just self pleasure."

"Oh no, you have it all wrong," said Ambrose. "All the Gods will be contributing to the minds and bodies of the people of the world. You have to consider the broad picture. You..."

"Yes, I can see pornography and no morals, running rampant all around the world, with her in charge," Nicole said sarcastically.

"No. You're not listening. They would not be in charge. They would be like an advisory council. The world would be getting the best from each of them, and with my discoveries here, we can turn this planet into a real Garden of Eden. Just think of the possibilities. There would always be an element of... let's say substandard minds, but they can be controlled with a negligible effect on society."

Nicole was almost in tears. "Uncle, why don't you trust me? Your secret is safe with me. When I first came here, I did not trust Merlin, or his staff. I almost called the authorities."

"I could not take a chance, no matter how slim, of someone accidentally revealing my secret, that I was alive. All our lives are at stake here. Professor Mundez was just one of many who seek out my discoveries. I am fortunate to have Merlin and the others who surround me with a security perimeter. You should place more trust in them. They are also protecting the four of you.

"Now that you know of my secret basement, you will have to visit me more often down here. I can't take the chance of being seen through a window while wandering around upstairs. I have plans to complete and strategies to forge. You should return to your studies. You and Merlin may have to continue my work, if I become indisposed."

"Uncle Ambrose, we are so happy you're back with us. We would like to be more helpful. We can do anything you want. Please, let us help."

"Yes, yes of course. But we can talk of that tomorrow, or at another time. Right now, I need time to think."

"Professor Hamlock, I think," started Cass as she came through the door backwards, carrying a lunch tray. "Oh, I'm sorry. I did not intend to interrupt. I'll put the tray here on the table and leave."

"Nonsense, Cass, I don't think you have met my niece, Nicole and her three friends, Dyllan, Travis and Austin. Everyone, this is Cass, my right hand. She is my indispensable second mind, keeping all this on an even keel."

Travis is mesmerized. Staring, he had only eyes and ears for Cass.

"Uncle," whispers Nicole "is she like the others?"

"Yes and no. Yes, she has been re-created and no, she is not a god. Cass is my ultimate achievement being created as an original. She has the best traits of all, and void of any bad. She is my conscience, confidant and sounding board."

"I do what I can for your uncle," said Cass.

"We had better leave you to your work," said Nicole.

The four leave Professor Hamlock and Cass. Cass said, "They impress me professor. I can see a lot of you in your niece Nicole. The two boys are a little immature and have a tendency to stare, but I believe

115

they will grow out of that. Anyway, that is what I have read about the differences between the two genders."

"Yes, they do outgrow their immaturity and juvenile traits, don't they? They have a reason to stare at you Cass. You are a beauty to behold. If I were younger I feel staring at you would be a pleasurable time for me. You should take that stare as a compliment of your exquisite being.

"I am proud of my niece. She is becoming a good asset to our endeavors. I will have to speed up her training to take over for Merlin. The time difference from his past life to now still bewilders him. I expect too much from him and can tell that the lack of human contact for all those years is a burden on him."

## Chapter 21

Aphrodite, Athena, Artemis and Adonis sit in the library discussing their perceived role in this new world they are part of. "Here we are, Gods of Legend, and we are treated with less respect than that given to the humans. What good are we? What will we be in the professor's grand scheme of things? We would be better received, passing ourselves off as humans. We have to ally ourselves to each other with a common goal of what is best for us," said Artemis.

"That's it! We have to become humans. Now, we are scared to reveal ourselves because of the unknown reaction," said Aphrodite.

"That is a good idea, but how can we become as common people? We need to observe the humans in their natural habitat. We will have to leave here unobserved and function in their world to become believable. I feel we can best accomplish this individually, and then consolidate our findings to achieve the maximum exposure in the shortest time," said Athena.

"Careful, we must be careful and cautious to not alert anyone of what we are doing. Merlin keeps a watchful eye on us. No more than two of us at a time should venture forth, while the remaining two can distract Merlin from becoming aware of our plans," said Adonis

"Wait. How do we know where to go for observing? We have to find a way to ease into their world. Maybe we can talk Professor Hamlock, or Merlin to take us on tours of sort, and explain the customs to us, their way of thinking and the premises of their interactions. We will have to approach them with a credible reason for observing and learning. We will need to better understand the human mind in order to facilitate decisions in running the world, to make everything function smoother between the regions of this time. Yes, this is what we will do," said Athena.

Artemis sits back; chin in hand, deep in thought. "Forget Merlin. He would be too suspicious. We need to convince the professor, and Cass. First we will convince Cass to approach the professor, but in a way where she will think it's her idea, that we should be orientated to this time with the perspective of the ordinary people. We must poise our thoughts to be neutral, letting her think of the positive rationale to our quest. Yes, Cass has to be the one to approach the professor. He has a high respect for her thoughts and logic.

But who is the right one to approach her with the idea. Maybe Adonis. Do you think she would succumb to his charm?"

"I don't think she thinks too highly of me. She does not look at me when I talk to her, not like she looks at you Artemis. She respects you and looks into your eyes when you speak. You should be the one to approach her," said Adonis.

Artemis lowers her head, her eyes focused on the floor, and then raises her gaze to Adonis. "I cannot tell an untruth. If I were to approach Cass it would have to be with an open heart. If she cannot be swayed to our cause logically, then another messenger must be sent."

"No," said Athena. "You are the one best to approach Cass. Remember, she is not a God. She is endowed with the intelligence from the best of humans and would soon realize that she is being maneuvered with half-truths and lies of omission. Artemis, you will have to approach her with truth and an honest heart, but we must prepare the message to best light our quest correctly. She must see what our light reveals. I believe the most opportune time to approach Cass is after breakfast, when she meditates in the garden. Her mind will be void of complex thoughts brought on by Professor Hamlock's strategies and more into a nurturing frame. She will have to believe that we would be better guidance counselors to the humans, with the required empathy, if we can humanize ourselves. Yes, Artemis, you are the messenger and now we must prepare the message."

## Chapter 22

Merlin sat at the table opposite Professor Hamlock. He treasures these moments with his friend, enjoying a glass of spirits and engaging in thought provoking conversation. Cass had brought a tray of cordials, Black Raspberry and Hypocras, a strawberry flavored mead. He thought the Hypocras was the better of the two. Cass sits in an easy chair away from the table, but within hearing range. If it were not for the drink in her hand, she would appear to be asleep. Observing her, he noticed her smile whenever the professor praised an action she had taken. *Spoiled, completely spoiled*, he thought. *She is a servant and not in the same league with the Gods and myself. She would soon learn to be a proper worker under my guidance.*

Aphrodite and Athena quietly enter the game room. "What do you think would do the most damage and not be easily noticed?" said Aphrodite.

"Anything we do will be noticed. We'll just have to make it look like one of the house staff had a clumsy accident. Just look around and maybe it will come to us. Maybe throwing water on the equipment will work?" said Athena. "When Merlin or the professor manipulates the controls, he does not even look to see what he is doing. We could realign the controls to corrupt the input and maybe cause a break down."

"No he is concentrating on the registers, and the gauges that he watches constantly while he re-creates," responded Aphrodite. "We have to be very careful to point any suspicion away from us. A little encouragement from us could draw the four humans here to experiment without Merlin or the professor condoning their actions. We will have to implant a reason or a being for them to center their minds on, treasures, or a goddess for the men and a god for the women? No, I think a source of food to feed the world. Yes, that would do it. Appeal to their sense of goodness. We will have to work fast to set a trap that they will encircle themselves in."

Professor Hamlock sits sipping his drink, occasionally looking over to Cass. *Someday she will be a brilliant companion to a lucky young man.* Cass should be given more exposure to the thinking, slang and dress of the modern youth. She is much too mature for her age. His thoughts rambled through the occupants of his dwelling. Merlin must also be brought up to date on the customs and language of today's society so he can interact more effectively.

Merlin is thinking of what he must do to manage the gods in council under his tutelage. Now he must work on completing a plan for immortality. *I know there is no potion or spell to accomplish living forever, but maybe the professor's equipment can do it. My questions to further understand the machines cannot reveal my real motives, a quest for immortality and re-create Niviane to exact my revenge on her. She will suffer as I, while imprisoned in that black rock, while I will not allow her to die. She will become insane, knowing the why and how of her infinite incarceration. I know my revenge will not reflect what a better being should do, but pain still lingers in my heart without relief until this deed be done.*

Aphrodite and Athena walk through the game room, sliding their hands over the equipment, looking for a crucial part to sabotage. Nothing found could satisfy the level of damage wanted. Aphrodite came to the chamber of life and knelt to the cover over the circuitry. Opening the box, she observes the wires with the connectors attached to the lugs. "Athena, come quick. I think the solution is here." With Athena watching over her shoulder, she switches wire connections. We have to remember which wires are switched, so they may be returned to their original positions. "We must return to the others and report what we have done," said Aphrodite.

Returning to the library, Aphrodite and Athena found Adonis and Artemis waiting for their return. "Have you done it?" whispered Artemis. "Are you sure it will work?"

"Yes," said Aphrodite. "We must be careful to express surprise at the next re-creation attempt."

"What will happen?" asked Adonis.

"We don't know, but I don't think a re-creation will materialize."

At this time, Dyllan, Nicole, Austin and Travis enter the room, looking suspiciously at the four gods. "We have to find out what they're up to," whispers Nicole. "They're just too chummy now and just yesterday they were at each other tooth and nail."

Merlin enters the library and said, "Nicole, who should we re-create tonight?

"Persephone," said Nicole. "Yes, Persephone would be a good addition to the Gods."

Merlin hesitates momentarily, trying to unravel the logic and purpose behind Nicole's choice. He also considers all the aspects in a re-creation of Persephone due to her love affair with Adonis and the possible conflict her presence could bring. "Good, we will bring her here. I am sure there is one who will be pleased with her company. Why wait until tonight when we can do the deed now?"

Adonis looks in horror to Aphrodite, Artemis and Athena. He secretly yearns for Artemis, but also has the seeds from his ancient love of Persephone in his heart. He cannot voice opposition to the re-creation because of what might happen to her, or counter the possible rekindling of an old love that might reveal their guilt. He did not know what he should do. Aphrodite, Artemis and Athena looked at Adonis, wanting to comfort him in his dilemma, as the results of their sabotage are unknown.

Merlin looks over the assembled group and asks, "Is there anyone else who would like to join us for the re-creation?"

"Yes," said Adonis. "I would like to welcome Persephone to this world. Maybe my presence will help ease her into this time of wonderment."

"Anyone else?" said Merlin. "No? Then come along Adonis, you can help. Your insight and knowledge of Persephone will make for an accurate rendition of a true entity."

*Maybe I can prevent or correct a mishap. Maybe nothing will go wrong. Maybe I can delay this until Aphrodite and Athena can undo their damage,* thought Adonis. "Merlin, must this be done now while we are so tired? Let us rest for a while and then begin the process. There is no hurry. I could use some time to list all the wonderful attributes Persephone has. We also cannot omit any of her beautiful physical or intellectual features."

"No, I may have other commitments this evening. I have everything needed in my book. Everything will be read out loud for your sanctions before we finalize. Come, we must begin," said Merlin.

Adonis follows with a heavy heart, a worry that could not be dispelled.

Merlin quickly enters the data from the detailed information in his book. Double-checking the compatibility checklist, he asked Nicole and Adonis, "Does everything seem correct. Is there anything you want to re-check or change before we begin?"

"No," they said in unison.

Merlin throws levers and pushes the hologram button. Persephone slowly rotated in the cloudy upright chamber. Gauges, digital readouts and sine waves are checked. "Last chance to correct anything," shouts Merlin above the ambient noise. The finalize button is depressed. In the chamber of life, a flash of lightning arcs through a foggy mist.

A delicate form begins to materialize. A breath catches in Adonis' throat and a tear gently rolls down his cheek. A large smile forms on his face and his eyes light up in recognition.

He starts to slowly walk toward the chamber to welcome the new arrival. Merlin stands watching his instruments in disbelief. *Something is wrong.* A fiery implosion, fed by the oxygen rich air, starts to consume Persephone. Writhing in pain, her body arches, looks at Adonis in recollection, and then slumps down as flames devour her body. Adonis looses all feeling in mind and body. His knees weaken and heart falters. A loud anguished scream echoes throughout the mansion.

Nicole cannot move, frozen in a standing position, not understanding what happened.

Merlin does not comprehend, still lost in reading his instruments. Mentally double checking everything he had done in the procedure. His mind cannot believe that he did something in error.

Aphrodite, Athena and Artemis cringe upon hearing Adonis scream. Dyllan, Austin and Travis run toward the game room, with the three gods trailing.

Entering the game room they encounter a dense black overwhelmingly sickening sweet blanket of impenetrable smoke. Dyllan called out, "Nicole, are you alright?"

Aphrodite calls out, "Merlin is everything O.K.?"

Artemis calls out, "Adonis, this way. Come to my voice."

Merlin, Adonis and Nicole break through the thick cloud coughing, eyes watering and their skin covered with a thin soot like coating. Adonis and Nicole are crying while Merlin looks bewildered.

Dyllan, Austin and Travis encircled Nicole, trying to comfort her with hugs and soothing sounds. Aphrodite, Athena and Artemis pull Adonis away from the smoke and down the hallway with questioning looks. Merlin collapsed against the wall. "I have to tell Ambrose. He has to know what just happened," he shouts to himself out loud. He had already thrown the exhaust fan switch and fresh air is already voiding the room of the putrid sweet smoke.

Dyllan, Austin and Travis half pulls and carries Nicole back to her room for a shower and change of clothing. Merlin steadies himself before rushing off to find Professor Hamlock. Aphrodite, Athena and Artemis quietly question a mute Adonis, getting no answers, and then cautiously return to the game room.

Aphrodite locates the electrical box, returning the wire connectors to their original positions. Wiping the smudge marks off the box, they then help Adonis to his room to shower and change clothing. Returning to the library they order a drink to cleanse their throats of the foul airborne contaminates. Adonis remains in a stupor not hearing, nor responding, to verbal questions.

Merlin crashes through the basement doors. Entering Professor Hamlock's sub-basement quarters, he startled the professor and Cass. Interrupting their intense conversation, Merlin said, "We had an accident. I was trying to re-create Persephone. There was an implosion and she burned to death. She was totally consumed by the fire while she was conscious. Adonis is catatonic and Nicole's friends are attending to her.

I saw something was wrong, but could not react in time to prevent the horror. I feel I did something wrong, but could not find how, even after rerunning the process in my mind several times. We should investigate the cause immediately to determine malfunction or my error. I do not think I can withstand Adonis looking at me, like he did, again."

Cass was visibly upset. "Ambrose, you have to go immediately. Everyone will need a comforting hand

and will look to you for guidance. I will prepare the household staff and have them ready the appropriate spirits to dull their pain and medications to ward off mental anguish. I think both will be needed to rest their bodies and minds before morning."

Merlin and Professor Hamlock hastily returned to the game room. Inspecting the equipment and running an analytic program produced no negative results. Then running a history-analyzing program found a wiring malfunction severe enough to produce the calamity described by Merlin. Tracing the wiring circuit brought Professor Hamlock to the box where the wiring connectors were switched. Black smudge covered everything but the box cover. He could not believe someone would purposely subvert the equipment and for whatever reason. He confided in Merlin what he had discovered. "Why Merlin, why would anyone do this? Call in the household staff to clean the equipment and we will rerun the process," said Professor Hamlock.

Merlin calls in the cleaning staff and supervises them in returning the room to its previous pristine condition. Then Professor Hamlock re-enters Merlin's previous data input. Pushing the finalize button produces a remarkably beautiful maiden that was everything described in ancient writings. Merlin and Professor

Hamlock do not fully notice her beauty, as they were more engaged in the technical aspects of the re-creation.

After verifying that everything correctly processed, they approach Persephone resting on the slide out rail, taking everything in. She listens, smells, tastes, breathes and mentally processes all her senses intake. Warily watching the two men approach, she stiffens in apprehension. A slight whimper escapes her throat.

Professor Hamlock speaks softly, "Persephone, do you remember anything?"

"Yes, I remember returning to Hades."

"And how do you feel?"

"Refreshed, but I do not know you or where I am."

"My name is Professor Hamlock and this is Merlin. You are in the year 2016. You are here with other Olympus Gods and Merlin to help the people of this time. Do not be afraid. Our first action will be to clothe you."

Persephone looks down at herself and with a gasp tries to cover herself with her hands, bringing her knees up into a fetal position. Merlin did not realize that she was so modest, unlike the other Gods. Professor Hamlock quickly covers her with a laboratory coat, helps her to her feet, and leads her to the wardrobe. "You will find appropriate clothing here with all required accessories. The wardrobe doors will provide cover from view for you. We will walk away and when you are dressed, step out and we will talk. If you have any questions about the clothing or accessories, call out and we will be ready with answers to your questions."

Persephone looks at Merlin and Professor Hamlock with suspicion but seeing she had no alternative, complies. Questions about the underclothing, footwear and accessories are asked and answered. When Persephone finally finished dressing and steps out from behind the door, Merlin and Professor Hamlock are taken with her beauty. Both have to forcibly control themselves not to stare. Professor Hamlock looks at her hair, Merlin her hands and making eye contact only when speaking to her. "Now we can talk. First, we will answer your immediate questions. Then we will inform you of where and why you are here, and explain who and what we are."

Persephone looked perplexed, taking a deep breath asked, "Who are you and what do you want of me."

"I am Professor Ambrose Hamlock. I made all this machinery that brought you here. My associate is Merlin. He is a famous magician who died long ago, and I re-created him in this time for the same purpose you are here. Adonis is also here. Together…"

"Adonis is here? He is here now? Oh I must see him. I need him by my side now. Will you please summon him?"

"Yes, Merlin will call for Adonis to come here."

Merlin picks up a cell phone, calling a member of the house staff to bring all the Gods to the game room.

"The Gods will be here shortly," said Merlin

"What other Gods are here?" said Persephone.

"Aphrodite, Athena and Artemis," said Professor Hamlock. "I must tell you that Merlin and I are quite taken with your beauty and you must excuse us if we seem to stare. We are trying not to be impolite."

"Me, I am not beautiful. From my reflections of past times, I must say I am quite plain."

"Nonsense, come with me." Merlin escorts Persephone to the rotating platform surrounded with mirrors. "Look and see your beauty."

Persephone blushes as she views herself from every possible angle. "I, I am not plain. I have never seen myself like this before."

Professor Hamlock stops the rotating platform. "Come and sit, we will continue our talk."

Persephone hesitates, looking back over her shoulder at the mirrors. "Yes."

Sitting Persephone down, Professor Hamlock continues the conversation, with Merlin nodding in agreement to his statements.

A staff member knocks on the door where Adonis had just finished dressing. He is still in a stupor with the other Gods trying to cheer him. "Merlin and Professor Hamlock requests that all of you return to the game room. They want you there immediately. We will escort you."

The four Gods give each other a helpless look. They feel as guilty as they look, each feeling a dread of what will come. Adonis comes out of his stupor when he hears the request. He cannot imagine what judgment will be pronounced when meeting the professor and Merlin. *I deserve whatever is given.*

Entering the game room produces a change in their demeanor as they see Persephone sitting enjoying the attention of Merlin and Professor Hamlock. Persephone leaps up and runs to Adonis, clutching him tightly. Adonis forcibly pulls her away so he could look at her. "You're alright. You're beautiful, you're alive."

"Yes, isn't this wonderful, we are together again."

"Merlin, how?" asks Adonis.

"The professor and I found the problem and corrected it, and then re-created Persephone again. She has no memory of the horrible accident."

"Accident? What accident?" asked Persephone.

Merlin paused, thinking of an appropriate response. "There was a small problem on our first attempt to re-create you. There is nothing for you to worry about. Everything has been corrected and now, you are a wonderful and beautiful asset to this gathering of minds. You have much to learn of this time. Everything you know from your past is useless in application here, except for the evaluation of the individual."

Persephone looks at Adonis while digesting Merlin's response. "Adonis, you look somewhat culpable. What is the matter? Why do you not look at me?"

Adonis does not realize that his guilt is reflected on his face. "I was remorseful in the thought of your possible pain from the accident. Now I can see your health and intellect is as it should be.

## Chapter 23

Professor Hamlock studies Merlin's face. "Merlin, I think it is time to re-create Professor Mundez."

"I do not relish the thought of his presence, he annoys me, and how would he be explained? Knowledge of his return would jeopardize you and your mission."

"Yes, he does get under one's skin."

"Under my skin? I do not understand. How does he get under my skin?"

"That is a figure of speech Merlin. It means his presence irritates you mentally. It means you do not feel comfortable near him."

"Oh yes. That is it exactly. I do not like him. I do not like his look. I do not like his smell. I do not like his words. I do not like his effect on others or myself. Yes, I do not like him."

"Come and we will make adjustments to his psychic."

Merlin follows Professor Hamlock with reluctance. The distance between the two widened until the Professor stops to let Merlin catch up. A slight smile came to the Professor's mouth. "Merlin, you are not intending to take another path to avoid participating in this re-creation, are you?"

"No. I hopefully thought maybe a plan would formulate in me to change your mind. This is a distasteful thing you are about to do. How can you reconcile this action after what he did? He murdered you and now you are giving him back life. I can think of a thousand others more suitable, with more to contribute, than that dreg of humanity."

"Come Merlin. You know I always have a plan. Come help me design a new personality for this one. I believe we can build a mind that you can appreciate."

Entering the laboratory, the Professor and Merlin set to work making an outline of a new Professor Mundez, then began to fill in the minute, but necessary, details.

"He must be a free thinker in order to achieve originality. And, he has to have a worthwhile ego to achieve his elevated goals. But, we must diminish his malicious attributes and make him more compassionate to others. We will also have to correct his heart condition. We can't have him immediately dying from the stress of rebirth." With a little chuckle, Hamlock returns to his calculations. Reviewing his lists of traits, he begins to input his data.

"Wait," said Merlin. "Can we at least give him ugly yellow and crooked teeth, crossed eyes and a crooked nose, or even a stutter?"

"Merlin. That is beneath you. He will be a different person, one that will be very likeable. He must possess tremendous self confidence to fulfill the demands that will be placed on him."

"Yes, I know. It's just that I will still remember him as he was."

Finishing his data input, the Professor engages the review process and studies the hologram as it forms in the cloudy mist and rotates in the upright glass cylinder. Even in this non-animated view, the image, and the memory it provokes, makes him hesitate. Then with a faltering thought, he presses the *Finish* button. Miniature arcs of lightning highlight the image as it solidified in the chamber of life. Finished, Professor Mundez slides out through the foot of the chamber, with a gaseous hiss, creating an oxygen rich airflow that circulates throughout the room.

Professor Hamlock walks to the opposite side of Professor Mundez and leans over to study the being lying before him. Merlin looks down with a scowl critical of everything he views. Mundez takes a sharp breath, and then slowly opens his eyes to see Merlin. His eyes open wide in fear, and then shifts his eyes to see Hamlock. "Dead. You're dead. Am I in hell? Am I also dead?" His body experiences a heavy shiver and he clinches his eyes as if in pain. "No. No. I don't want this."

"You're O.K. Professor Mundez. You are alive and healthy. Let me help you up." Grasping his hands, Hamlock pulls a resisting Mundez up to a sitting position. "Take a deep breath and relax. Merlin and I have brought you back."

Mundez stares at Hamlock then turns his head toward Merlin. "What have you done? How did you do this? Where am I? Why…."

Hamlock raises his hand to interrupt Mundez. "Relax. Everything will be explained. Do you remember the events of our death?"

"Yes. And now I am in fear of what I have done."

"Good. That means you know what you did was wrong and now fear retribution. But, no, there will be no retribution. Now we must clothe and feed you. Your body needs nourishment and comfort."

Merlin helps Hamlock raise Mundez to his feet and escorts him to the wardrobe. He is not taken to the rotating platform with the mirrors. After dressing, Mundez is taken to the dining room and fed. He is not served tea, but a dark, strong hot coffee. There are no more questions to further agitate him.

Mundez looks at everything, analyzing his surroundings. He feels his intellect is sharper and the information he is gathering is easier to decipher and categorize. Finishing his meal and enjoying the linger time over the coffee, he begins what he thinks, is the interrogation by Hamlock who smiles at his attempt to gain the upper hand in their first battle of their minds.

"Professor Hamlock. What just happened? Why do I feel different but yet the same? How can you be here?"

"All your questions will be answered. First of all, you were just re-created. Merlin and I have brought you back with my equipment that you had previously sought. You feel different because we made a few adjustments to you, but you are basically the same as before, just as I am here because Merlin re-created me after you poisoned me with your *rare* tea.

You are here to help me make the world a better place for all to live. I think you need time to rest. Tomorrow all your questions will be answered."

Mundez is taken to his room where he sits reviewing the situation. *I must be missing something here. Why did that idiot bring me back? Do I have some knowledge that is crucial to him and why is that imbecile imposter Merlin here? I must prepare a plan to regain everything that was lost when he killed me. I must use his own ego to rid myself of interference from his cronies and himself. His Achilles heel must be hidden from me right there in plain sight. Tomorrow, yes tomorrow a plan will come to me. Yes, tomorrow will be the beginning of his demise.*

**Chapter 24**

Sitting at a table in the library, Aphrodite looks at Athena, Artemis, Adonis and Persephone with a concerned look. "What do you think? Should we place this Professor Mundez under surveillance? I don't think Professor Hamlock thought it through before bringing that murderer back. I for one do not trust him. Artemis, tell us what you think?"

"His eyes are too close together and his eyes seem to lie to his own face. He apparently was not to be trusted before and he is not to be trusted now. Persephone, you are the newest to our group. You have dealt with evil for almost all of your existence. What are your feelings about him?"

"I have seen that same self absorbed look, many times, in Hades. The damned have that same sneer of a smile, and those eyes can only be backed with sinister thoughts. Yes, I agree, he cannot be trusted. I feel he will kill again. We will have to watch him carefully for any signs of malicious action. We should prepare a schedule to observe him. We each should be assigned to follow him at irregular intervals so he does not become suspicious. We should also be ready to intercede if it appears Professor Hamlock seems to be ready to show him the secrets of this house. Athena, this is more in your area of expertise. Why don't you prepare a schedule and assign us by the time of day and our different abilities to best accomplish this endeavor."

"Yes, I can do that, and Artemis, you can help me. Tomorrow we will begin. He may have to suffer an accident if he cannot be controlled. Happy is not a word to describe our Professor, if our plans are found out."

Dyllan and her three friends linger over the last of their pastries and morning coffee. "I think we should approach Merlin and Cass to get them to side with us. This Professor Mundez is not to be trusted. Together, I think we can sway Uncle Hamlock to send him back to the hell he was re-created from. I don't care what precautions they incorporated into his re-birth, you just can't counter, or remove evil with a few changes to his personality. I really fear for my uncle's safety. Nicole, you have influence with Merlin and Cass. They will listen to you. We need their knowledge and allegiance. I think you should approach Cass first and appeal to her sense of protection for your Uncle, and then once she is on board, she can work on Merlin. Merlin already has major distaste for that Mundez. In fact, he might just find a way to take care of that killer himself."

Professor Hamlock peers at Merlin and Cass through the rising steam of his tea. He softly blows a cooling breath across his cup, a habit established in his youth. "Merlin, do you still think I made a tactical error in resurrecting Mundez?"

"Yes. I believe he is plotting now, to eliminate, or at least to diminish the power you hold. If he can find a way to take your life, to replace you, he will try it."

"Cass, what do you think? Can he be made to be trusted? Can he be molded into an ally?"

"No. I agree with Merlin. He cannot be trusted, nor remade to be trusted."

"Merlin, Cass, keep a close eye on him. If he looks like he is about to make a bad move, alert us, then make yourself scarce. Use your cell phone. We need to keep on top of this situation and keep ourselves safe. I feel an obligation to give him a second chance, but not at the price of hurting one of us."

Professor Mundez lays on his bed, deep in thought. *I must learn all about this house, it's contents, the people living here and everything about the people living here. This is like something out of a fantasy science fiction story. Even the memory of how I came to be here questions my sanity. I'll wait for everyone to go to sleep before I look around. There has to be something for me to find around this crazy place to explain what's going on. I may be able to interrogate one of those dimwit house staff. I don't think anyone in this funny house is playing with a full deck, especially Professor Hamlock and that weirdo wannabe Merlin.*

## Chapter 25

Nicole watches as Travis mindlessly re-arranges the silverware on the table. "Travis, I think you should engage Professor Mundez in a light conversation, to see what you can learn of his mind set. Try to feel him out. Let himself reveal his inner ambitions."

"Are you kidding? That guy is creepy. I try to avoid being anywhere near him. You engage him to expose his mind".

"Austin, you're not bothered by his presence. You feel him out, or whatever."

"Me? If he looks at me wrong, I just might smack him in the head. Dyllan, why don't Travis and you gang up on him? Travis can be a distraction while you engage in conversation. He may get confused and let something slip. Hell, I get confused when I am stuck between the two of you when you're talking to each other."

"Maybe we should talk with Uncle Hamlock before we do anything." Said Nicole.

Athena finds Aphrodite sitting in the library, head back, eyes closed, listening to music with an open book on her lap. A gentle snore underscores the music with less than favorable contribution to the score. Her mouth is slightly open and a little drop of spittle is just ready to roll off her lower lip to her chin. Athena finds the scene showing a vulnerability of Aphrodite's beauty and mystic, but also a child like facet of her. "Aphrodite, wake up. We have matters to discuss."

Aphrodite wakes startled and gives a quiet snort. Her tongue flicks out to capture the bead of spittle. The face that brought legions of men to their knees shows an embarrassment, tinged in pinkness. "Athena, you startled me. I fell asleep listening to the music and was dreaming of…. Well I was dreaming of a time, in a language, from long ago. In my dream I felt a longing for that time and place. I believe I am just plain homesick. What do we need to talk about?"

"I want to talk more about creating an opportunity to study the humans. I have been thinking a lot about this lately and I feel we should accompany the four young mortals for our observations and exposure to this time. I haven't talked to the others about this and want to hear what you thought about this strategy."

Aphrodite's eyes are still glazed, her mind slow from her nap, and mulls over what Athena had just said. "I think that is a wonderful plan. We could split into two groups with each accompanying one of the couples. What excuse should we use to encourage them to be receptive to our plan?"

"I think the best way is to get Merlin, or Professor Hamlock to suggest it. I propose we present the idea to them in a most innocent manner. We Gods needs to better understand the mortals and what they think. We need to be able to mingle amongst them unnoticed and in order to do that we will need a mantle of disguise. We will need the four of them to help change our speech and attire, making us invisible in plain sight. Perhaps Merlin has something in his bag of tricks for us."

"Aphrodite, I think we should just plant the seed to grow in their minds. Let them tell us what they think, while we can be selective in what we feel would be best for us. Letting them make the suggestions will prevent any suspicion of what we want to accomplish."

Artemis and Persephone enter the library seeing Aphrodite and Athena engaged in conversation, their heads close and voices lowered. "I am sorry. Did we interrupt anything?" said Persephone.

"No, not at all. We were just planning how we can maneuver observation trips among the mortals for all of us. You have come at a most desirable time." Replied Aphrodite. Athena repeats their complete discussion to the new arrivals and they nod their heads in agreement.

"Now who should approach Merlin with this idea. I think Persephone is best thought of in Merlin's mind. What do you think?" Said Athena.

Persephone looks at Athena for a few moments before answering. "I believe that approaching both Merlin and Professor Hamlock, at the same time would be best. I could possibly play one against the other in discussion over the merits of our idea, letting them pick up the thought and enhance the possibilities in it. We may even be able to have Merlin escort us and be a sounding board to better understand what we see. Maybe even Professor Hamlock. It may be conducive to suggest Cassidy join us. She also needs exposure to this time of expanded experience."

## Chapter 26

Persephone finds the Professor Hamlock and Merlin deep in discussion about improving the re-creation process in light of Professor Mundez's outcome. "Professor, I have a request to make. We have talked of mingling with the mortals and would like your advice on when you think we will be ready for observations and where that would be best accomplished? We Gods believe we are ready for the endeavor and would like to know of any preparation you might think we need."

"Yes. Merlin and I have discussed this at length and we feel the university campus would be the perfect environment for that task. A Monday morning would be an excellent time for the initial contact."

"We would also like for Merlin and Cassidy to accompany us to ensure a smooth interaction. Also Merlin could be a buffer in the case of overly interested males. Their being young and possibly not possessing the social skills to properly interact."

"Merlin, what do you think? Would you be willing to take Cassidy with you to accompany the Gods, or do you feel the large assembly of intruders would be too noticeable on the campus? The individuals in our group may not fit in or mix well with the students on the campus. Although I could arrange for a group of visiting teachers to have access to the university's facilities, for an exchange of ideas. We would have to identify your fields of teaching. Hhhmmmmm – old English Culture, Greek Mythology, Ancient Hunting, Greek History, Greek Warfare, Psychology of Love, Agriculture; yes, we can cover everyone. Adonis, you of course, will have to be a Horticulturist. Yes. I believe we can, and will do this. Nicole and her friends will have to brief the group on body language and verbal articulation to enable conversation with the students without standing out.

Professor Mundez stands just outside the door, listening. *What are they up to? They are going to be very obvious, a group of older individuals standing around watching the students. I hope they get arrested.*

*That will keep them out of my hair, especially that charlatan Merlin. Then I can search that nightmare workshop they call the game room to see what can be found.*

## Chapter 27

Merlin, and his group commandeer a large gazebo in the center of the university's plaza. The air is fresh and the sterilized fruit trees are in full blossom. The stone paths are still damp from last night's rain. Students have to cross the plaza if transitioning buildings. Passing by, walkers could not help but notice the physical contrast between the geeks and the Gods. Aphrodite has to resist the urge to lounge on a bench. It was previously stressed to her that looking sultry and seductive was not in keeping to their objective. *It's hard to be constantly looking alert and proper.* She thought to herself. Instead, she just leaned back against the railing behind the bench. Not many stopped to talk, but most of those that did were curious young men drawn to them by beauty that could not be concealed by clothing.

"Are you students here?" Asked a male student, while trying to focus on Persephone. Merlin blocked the entrance to the gazebo, keeping the male student from stepping in.

"No. We are visiting teachers for an informal conference on teaching methods," responded Merlin. "We arrived early and are taking advantage of this fine weather."

"I would sure like to take your classes," he said, focusing on Aphrodite. "What do you teach?" He asked Aphrodite.

"Mental pre-conception contraceptive methods for the unaware," replied Aphrodite.

"Oh," said the young student with a lowered voice.

Athena spoke up. "I teach self defense and hand to hand combat for women."

"No thanks," said the young man. "I think general studies will be enough for me now. I was just thinking of a fill-in course for some extra credits. I don't think those courses would have a positive effect on my curriculum," as he turned to continue to his destination.

Nicole stifled a soft laugh. "Boy, you two catch on fast. That poor guy was cut off at the knees."

Merlin spoke up. "Aphrodite. What did you learn from that exchange of words? "

"That young mortal thought in the extreme short range. There was no planning before engaging in conversation and I could tell from his eyes and breathing that he did not have his collegiate education on his mind. His ultimate goal was shamefully apparent."

"I don't know. I thought he was kind of cute," said Artemis. "Really. Now you sound like Aphrodite," said Persephone.

Adonis is watching a tall, slim blonde approach them. She is holding two books pressed against her abundant bosom. A tight short sleeved white sweater and form fitting white slacks emphasize her figure. Her face rivals his companion Gods. Their eyes locked on each other. Her walk changes ever so slightly at the eye contact. Her face changes from a sun drench squint to a relaxed subtle smile with lips partially open, revealing pearl white teeth.

Stepping up to Merlin, she said sweetly. "Hello. My name is Summer, and I am gathering people for a forum to discuss student-teacher ratios, length of classes, and the availability of evening and weekend courses. And if at all possible, I would especially like to count on this group's attendance. It will be conducted off campus, this evening. The time and address are on these invitational cards."

Merlin reads the card out loud. "Dinner: Served at 6 p.m. followed by meeting 7 to 9:30 p.m. at the Carriage Inn on University Drive," on the card, as Summer is passing them out. Her hand lingers, as fingers touched, while offering Adonis a card. Her eyes open a fraction and lips purse ever so slightly. "I will be looking for you this evening," she whispers as she walks away.

Adonis has had uncountable encounters with beautiful women in his time, but Summer stands out from them. Sheepishly, he glances back to Persephone, to see if she noticed the brush of invitation. A frown and tightly set lips tells him she had. He quietly re-runs the past minute through his mind, stopping at the more enjoyable moments, until interrupted by Merlin. "Adonis, what do think of the young lady's invitation?"

Adonis is taken aback, not being sure to which proposal Merlin was referring. "I think her invitation was intriguing. Maybe we should attend to get a better feel for the political process being played out here on this campus."

"I think not," replied Merlin. "Her voice was not sincere and she did not look me in the eye when reciting her invitation."

"Well, she was looking me in the eye."

"Were you looking into her eyes and not just at her eyes?"

Aphrodite added to the conversation. "She did not look trustworthy to me. She did not look at me once, only to Adonis and that look was not for attending a forum. We female Gods could read what her invitation was for and it was not for group participation in the topic she professed."

The discussion of the offer was stopped, when another young female student approached. "What are you doing? Is this some kind of survey? Is this something to do with the rock concert next week?"

"No. We are visiting teachers, just out enjoying the weather before attending our conference," said Merlin.

"Oh," said the student, who then turned and walked away with a backward hungry glance at Adonis.

"I think observing the mortals during a period of interactive discussion would be very beneficial." Adonis offered.

"I have never heard of an off campus forum like that. It all sounds bogus to me," said Travis.

"I agree," said Austin.

"I have met and talked with every member of the student council and have never seen or heard of anyone like Summer," said Dyllan.

"We should go to the university cafeteria before it gets too crowded. Professor Hamlock gave me money to pay for our meals," said Nicole.

**Chapter 28**

Even at this early hour, the group of eleven had a difficult time finding a table large enough to accommodate them comfortably. "This food leaves much to be desired after eating at the Manor. I do not believe I can eat this," complained Aphrodite as she pushes away her tray and sets down her fork. Her eyes are locked onto an athletic built student still wearing his workout clothing. Her eyes drifted up and down as he approached. Smile and inviting eyes evaporate into a glare when he stops, a table short of them, to sit with three young girls. Leaning over to Persephone's ear, she whispers, " I cannot wait until I can enjoy their freedoms, and to marry and have a family. To be mortal." A small tear found it's way down her cheek.

"Aphrodite. What do you think?" Said Artemis.

"What? What did you say?" Replied Aphrodite.

"Weren't you listening? I said that this is a better place to observe. We don't look out of place here. What do you think?" Noticing Aphrodite's sad face, Artemis said. "Aphrodite is something wrong? You look as if something is wrong. Are you feeling O.K."?

"No, I'm fine. I was just deep in thought. I see all these happy young people, enjoying themselves and each other, and I feel emptiness in my existence. I would rather be like them, carefree, preparing myself for a better existence."

Merlin, seeing the turn of the group's focus said. "Alright, let's concentrate on why we are here. Aphrodite, try to eat some of your food. There is a lot of time until supper and we have yet to start taking note of our impressions. Nicole and Dyllan, you are not helping with the group. You are here to give direction and interpretation of what we see. Austin and Travis, go mingle and create some controversial conversation to determine the rationale of these young people. The rest of you, do what you do best, making eye contact and smiling to encourage interaction. I have seen better flirting from new born babies than from you."

Athena did what she thought was her best maneuver. She stuck out her foot to trip a nerdy looking male. The tray he carried flew out to land on a neighboring table causing food to explode over the six students silently studying while nibbling their food. Screams of surprise and cries of panic were uttered as peopled jump away to avoid the projectile food and hands with napkins tried to wipe away the splatters to no avail.

"Oh, I'm sorry. Let me help you up," proffered Athena. Pulling the young man to his feet, she wiped over the front of his pants, while gently pulling him against her breast for apparent balance. "You must allow me to replace your food. I am so clumsy." She said, her mouth inches from his. "What is your name?"

"Robert."

"Is that what your friends call you?"

"No, they call me Bob."

"Can I call you Bob?"

"You can call me anything you want." He watches her gaze go from his eyes to mouth, then back again. He has to step back to slide his view down her body and back to her eyes. His mouth goes dry and he feels a little disorientated as she pulls him back against her.

"Sit with me." She said while gently guiding him to a chair at a nearby table. She pulls another chair next to his and sat. "What would you like?"

"Like? What would I like? I would like to…"

"Food. What can I get you for the spilled food? I feel just a little responsible for your accident."

"Nothing. I'm not hungry anymore." He said while staring at her face. "What…what is your name?"

"Artemis. I am named after the Greek God of War."

"Is Artemis a girl's name?"

"Oh yes. And I am all girl."

"I can see that. Are you a student here, I hope?"

"No, but there is no reason why I could not be. Well Bob, what are you studying here? Something interesting I bet."

"Creative Writing, Creative Writing in the English Department."

"And why did you decide on that course of study?" Artemis continues questioning Bob on what he does and why he does it, while the rest of group continues drawing in people for their reaction. Dyllan watches Artemis' body language, with a cocked eye, while she grills Bob.

"*A cougar if I ever saw one,*" mumbles Dyllan to herself. Her attention is drawn back to the group as

Merlin directs their attention toward Austin and Travis as they socialize with a group sitting two tables away. They are talking *GEEK*, and with a louder higher pitched voice, Athena said. "I have no idea what they are talking about. Can someone translate?"

Dyllan responds. "Yes. They are discussing a better world wide inter-net that would repel any virus and would be self policing for content. Athena, would you like a more in depth translation of what they are talking about?"

"No. No thanks. I think an explanation would just confuse me more than I am now."

Merlin decided to call it a day and return to the manor. He could see the groups focus was deteriorating at a rapid pace. "O.K. everyone, let's return to the manor. We can return and finish this another day."

## Chapter 29

Returning to the Manor brought a sigh of relief to Merlin. "I did not realize how taxing this little venture would be on me."

Aphrodite laughs in a soft gentle way and said, "I don't know. This afternoon was fun and very enlightening. I think the male mortals were quite taken with us. Artemis was especially taken with her mortal. That young man would not be dismissed. She had to put a vexing eye on him and then he was still like a lovable little puppy being pushed away."

Artemis looks down before saying, "I feel terrible about that. He was so happy when I touched his hand. He would have believed anything I told him."

"And what did you learn from your experience with him?" said Merlin.

"If he is a reflection of the other male mortals, it seems that they all have lost their survival instincts when it comes to dealing with a female. The thought of mating removes all common sense from their minds and is replaced with a singular focus," responds Artemis.

"Not all," said Professor Hamlock, who has just entered the room. "You cannot apply a single observation to all men. Many males are very skilled in word play, and would have turned your little game back on you. It is good that your initial engagement was a simple exercise, and with less experienced people."

Artemis, feeling somewhat verbally chastised, responded "I believe I had everything in control. I would have not allowed his endeavors to go anywhere but where I intended. I was in complete control". Dyllan and Nicole look at each other with a cocked eyebrow and a knowing smile.

Aphrodite thought. *Yes. These mortal men cannot match the calculating mind of a female God. We have been manipulating the male species since his creation. History has recorded our superiority over them consistently since the beginning of time. Even the Bible records the superior mind of Eve over Adam, using nothing more than an apple and her wiles, to get him to do her bidding.* Nodding to herself she notices the professor looking at her as if he could read her mind. A chill courses through her body as a thought surfaced. *Can he possibly be able to read my mind? He did re-create me with his devilish machinery. Who knows what liberties he took inputting the data. I know he could not have revealed all to me.*

## Chapter 30

Professor Mundez is searching the game room for something he could use, something that would give him an advantage over Merlin and Professor Hamlock. *His call to Summer did not work out as planned. She had failed to entice everyone to the bogus forum. Their absence would have allowed him a longer time frame for a more intensive search. This will have to do.* A thorough examination of the file cabinets and bookshelves did not produce anything that he did not already know. Now he searched for hidden compartments or storage places. *I would have searched his living quarters in the sub-basement but that nosy Cass would have surely discovered me. I need to get rid of all the pesky deterrents that block my efforts.*

His eyes fall onto a maintenance manual sitting on the work platform. It looks well used and opening it reveals copious writing on the equipment corrections, updates and their results. Personal notes and observation entries fills the borders and notation pages. References to other completed changes and their effects were overwhelming unless one had knowledge of the whole intricate process. Thinking that the binder would be too large to conceal within his clothing, Mundez finds one of the nerd's cloth computer bags and pressed it into service to hide his misappropriation. After successfully reaching his quarters, he sits at his desk to devour the contents of the manual. His training and studies did not prepare him for what he read. He understood the end result, but the theories and equations are far above his comprehension. He fumed at the thought of being thwarted in his attempt to finally bring down his antagonist. *There has to be a way to take over and control this whole organization. Either the professor or Merlin, or both, will have to be removed, permanently, and have the household bow to my authority. Maybe holding Hamlock prisoner would be enough to pressure the others to do my bidding. The Gods, they are useless and Merlin is so devoted to that idiot genius he will be like putty in my hands. I should have researched Hamlock and his operation deeper before I killed him the first time. The second time around will be cleaner and much more rewarding.*

Unknown to Mundez, a comprehensive system of video cameras had been installed after the game room was sabotaged. His nefarious action, and escape to his quarters, were recorded and monitored by Cass. A wicked smile plays over her mouth as she watches his planning on the monitor. *Yes* shouted in her subconscious mind. Plans took seed and grew in her mind until a complete scenario plays out. Cass casually pings the tiny microphone implanted in Professor Hamlock's ear. She calmly and quietly relays her observation.

With a sad expression, Hamlock stops conversation with the nerds and the Gods. He had been hoping to rehabilitate Mundez, but he could now see the impossibility of that. He calls Merlin to the side and relays Cass's message.

Merlin's face reflects his feelings. Vindication, satisfaction and delight are showing on his face. He nods to Hamlock, excuses himself from the gathering, and makes his way to the game room.

On entering, he immediately sits at an unusual looking machine. There are no knobs, labels or identifying tags. A keyboard, a digital readout and a red LED light that looks like a mouth and two eyes on the large black box that is void of features and makes the equipment look sinister in appearance. Merlin slowly keys in data with no visible reference or method of typographical error correction. He hesitates momentarily, as if mentally concentrating and reviewing his entry. When the red LED light turns off he presses **enter**, and returns to the group.

Mundez is still sitting at the desk, contemplating his next action when he feels a tingling in his feet. He pulls his foot from his left shoe, but there is just an empty sock crumpled in the shoe, no foot, and his right foot is also missing. There is no pain, just a tingling, then numbness. The horror of what is happening freezes his senses. His eyes bulge and mouth stretches open. Hands try to crush the chair arms until the trembling limbs loose their strength. The sensation slowly travels up his legs to his waist. Each inch of progression seems an eternity. *No, this cannot be happening.*

A loud piercing, bone chilling, scream is heard thru the living quarters of the mansion. Mundez hears his own pleading moans as his upper body slowly slides down the chair back, the empty clothing gathering on the seat. Static electricity sparks and arcs through the air, and a honey-citrus aroma wafts through the room, disappearing out an air vent. Air rushing in to fill the vacuum, created by the dematerialization, gently stirs residual dust on the empty piled clothing.

Cass watches the dissolving Mundez on a monitor with a satisfied look. She pings the microphone in Merlin's ear. "It is done." Merlin stands and returns his attention to the group meeting, with a smile on his face.

"I think there will be extra dessert for everyone this evening." Said Merlin. Professor Hamlock looks at Merlin with a frown of disapproval. The others in the group look to Merlin for an explanation but none is offered. Hamlock clears his throat and makes an announcement. "Professor Mundez was operating outside his programmed parameters. I had thought we diminished his less than honorable instincts, when programming his traits while re-creating him. Apparently we failed and had to disassemble him. He is no longer with us. I think all will be more at ease and comfortable with this action."

Artemis studies Merlin's and Professor Hamlock's faces, then raising an eyebrow nods to Aphrodite. A quiet settles over the room and everyone has a satisfied look about them, like entering a cool walk-in reefer from a July afternoon heat. Austin looks around and said in an innocent voice, "Well then, I think we should have some fresh mango sorbet this evening."

## Chapter 31

As everyone is leaving the evening meal, Artemis asks Aphrodite to follow her outside. Sitting on a bench in the garden, Artemis asks, "Aphrodite, what do you think about Professor Mundez being dematerialized?"

"I feel much more secure with him gone. I always felt that he would have liked for all of us to disappear. Whenever he looked at me, my body chilled. His eyes were always evaluating, roaming over me with a look of evil. Yes, I am glad he is no longer with us."

Artemis looked off into the darkness. She returned her gaze to Aphrodite, "I have been reading modern books on business. We need to make a business plan for our 'Mount Olympus Organization' and we need it now. We must begin our journey for independence. I am fearful of Professor Hamlock and Merlin's neutral reaction to our wants and needs, but I feel we must follow through for our own sake".

"Do you believe it would be best to ask the Gods as a group, or individually, on what they want to do?"

"As a group. That should stimulate discussion and eliminate any thought of a hidden agenda. We must prepare our presentation to the professor and Merlin in the best possible light and show our intent is not adversarial. Maybe we can encourage Merlin to join us and then help meld our different journeys into one.

Merlin studies his benefactor in his sub-basement quarters before asking. "Now what do we do. Everyone was accepting of what we did, but after they review what happened, they will come to a realization that what happened to Mundez could possibly happen to them under different circumstances. We have to reassure them; no matter what happens, they will never be dematerialized.

Aphrodite and Artemis knock, then open Hamlock's door. Aphrodite's face is solemn and hesitates before speaking. "Professor Hamlock. We have been discussing our fate, all of us, and have decided that we would like to become mortal. We would always be part of your vision and do not wish to leave you. We also would like to form an organization that would best utilize our talents. Further we want to ask Merlin to join us or become your advisor to us."

Professor Hamlock's face saddened, "Why? Are you not happy here? Has Merlin or I done something wrong?"

"No. You have done nothing wrong. We have seen the mortals interact with each other. We have seen their happiness and sorrow and feel we will never experience what they have unless we too become mortal. Surely, with your magical machines, you could accommodate our desires without any detrimental effects. We would like to continue living with you and helping you in any way we can, but as Gods, we feel useless. There are no challenges or events to look forward to. We want to be your family experiencing everyday stresses and desires."

"Yes desires," said Artemis. "I can see the desires on the mortals faces and I am envious of what they feel."

"But you will age, and you will feel pain and disappointment. Being mortal will mean that death will eventually come," said Merlin.

"Death! I never thought about that," said Aphrodite. "And will I get wrinkled and old."

"My machines can stop your aging, and death from aging," said Professor Hamlock. "What of your organization? What did you have in mind?"

"We are thinking of some type of management consulting concern, where we can intervene to prevent or correct problems and criminal activity. We thought that with all the major and minor Gods and your machines to re-create and possibly make them mortal, if they wish, any problem could be prevented or corrected." Aphrodite continued, "We do not have a name for our organization, but we would like it to be here, close to new talent and advise from our mentor."

Merlin closed his eyes in thought, then said, "How about 'Mount Olympus Solutions – No Problem Too Big Or Too Small'"

Artemis said, "You must have read our minds. If we combine all our knowledge we can solve any problem, anywhere. Merlin, you would be a major asset to our group along with the professor and the four mortals. Merlin, do you have other suggestions?"

"Yes. We should schedule a daily round table to discuss this new endeavor. What about payment? What kind of payment will we be receiving for our services? Further, what will be the scope of our services? There are all manner of questions that must be answered before we can offer our services. We will have to consult with the professor before we get ahead of ourselves."

## Chapter 32

Nicole feels strangely out of place in the courtroom environment. Her probate lawyer, Nierburt Spring, that was provided for in Professor Hamlock's will is stating that Nicole is the professor's only living heir.

A Professor John Smith, the acting Director of Science for the university counters by stating that, " As the universities' representative legal proof that Miss Nicole Dorms is in fact the biological niece of Professor Hamlock must be provided. Further, it is believed that Professor Hamlock had university property in his possession at the estate. This belief is based on statements made to members of the faculty, on university research conducted at his estate." Professor Smith states that the university wants a detailed inventory of the estate, certified by the court, to satisfy their demands.

"Your Honor, does the university want, when they say a 'detailed inventory' a listing of all Professor Hamlock's dirty socks and other personal items?"

"I object to demeaning insinuation being presented by Mr. Spring. We want to eliminate any possibility that university property is being illegally harbored on the property in question."

"Well your Honor. I would think the university should have documentation showing ownership of the assets in question. Items of research quality must have a chain of provenance, such as copies of requisition, deliveries, installation, maintenance and so on. When Professor Hamlock referred to his research, I am thinking he was referring to his mental research, plied on blackboard and on paper with pencil to allow for corrections. Equipment for science research is not something to put in one's pocket for transport. It appears that the university did not think their demands through, or they are simply on a fishing expedition to acquire knowledge written down by a genius. They do not even specify or hint on what kind of research they are contending. Before Professor Hamlock's death, his replacement, Professor Mundez did not pursue any requests of disclosure.

If anyone knew of research conducted by Professor Hamlock, off campus, it would have been Professor Mundez, as the two were very close, and conferred frequently. If the university can come up with some tangible record of the research or of the equipment they are referring to, I am sure accommodations can be made. But, I am not conducive to unfounded claims. It appears to me that Professor Smith is attempting to plunder a private estate for self serving reasons."

"Professor Smith, do you have a response to Mr. Springs statement?"

"Yes, your Honor. Mr. Spring is not considering the laws concerning intellectual properties and who owns them."

"Professor Smith. Do you have any notarized statements, affidavits or depositions to enter into the proceedings?"

"No your Honor. But I am sure once you consider the possible importance of Professor Hamlock's current science research, and the magnitude of his past discoveries to the United States, I am sure you will rule in our favor."

"Mr. Spring. Do you have anything to add before I declare my decision?"

"No your Honor. I believe my previous response is adequate."

"With nothing more to present to this court, I declare this probate hearing concluded and in favor of Miss Nicole Dorms. The will shall be carried out as written. Miss Dorms will inherit Professor Hamlock's estate in its entirety. This will is closed and the proceeding is adjourned."

The judged left the bench and Nicole plopped down with a sigh of relief. Leaving the courtroom, Professor Smith stops by Nicole's side. "This is not over young lady. The university is not going to loose what is rightfully theirs. Do not get attached to the mansion and it's contents."

Mr. Spring jumps to his feet. "Professor Smith. You are an out-and-out scoundrel. Be advised that I will not take any future atrocious actions like this lightly. I will be informing the court of your unprofessional comments and threats." To Nicole, he said, "Forget his threats Nicole. He has nothing in his make believe arsenal that can hurt you. His claims do not have a leg to stand on. Go home and remember your uncle. Enjoy what he has provided for you. Call me if there is anything else I can do for you. Good day."

## Chapter 33

Arriving back at the mansion, Nicole excitedly tracks down her Uncle Hamlock in the library. "Your will has been successfully probated. Professor Smith did threaten me with some kind of further action, but Mr. Spring pretty well shot him down and told him he is going to report him to the court."

"Tell me, what did Professor Smith say to you?"

"I believe his exact words were, "This is not over young lady. The university is not going to loose what is rightfully theirs. Do not get too attached to the mansion and it's contents. He had also referred to something called the laws of intellectual properties."

"That man, Smith, is an idiot. I have never met a person with so much excrement between the ears. He will never carry through with his threats unless someone in the university's hierarchy backs him up and I can't think of anyone that would do that. We have nothing to fear." Seeing Merlin come into the room Professor Hamlock said, "Merlin. Take Cass with you and visit the university. Nose around and try to find any information on why Professor Smith was trying to contest my will and if anyone is backing him. Take the Mercedes now that you've received your driver's license. And be careful on the road."

Merlin leaves searching out Cass, mumbling about the professor's lack of confidence in his skills behind the wheel.

Nicole sees Dyllan walk past the open door and shouts out to her. "Dyllan, I have good news. Wait up." Then rushed to the door to tell her about the outcome of the probated will.

"The will has been probated, isn't this great news."

"I don't know who I am most happy for, you or Professor Hamlock."

"All of us silly. Let's get the group together for a little celebration. Now we don't have to worry or keep looking over our shoulder."

"Oh, I think we will still have to do that. There are just too many people lurking out there waiting to get something for nothing. Where is everyone, maybe the library?"

Nicole and Dyllan find the rest of the group in the library in groups of two or three. Artemis is the first to notice Nicole and Dyllan enter the room. "Nicole, how did everything go?"

"Great. I came to tell everyone the news. The court ruled in my favor and the probate is closed."

Professor Hamlock enters the library just as Nicole finished telling her news. "We are not as safe as we may think. The university still wants access to my holdings. Some one on the faculty is determined to get my research notes and equipment. Our vigilance must be kept on high alert for intruders or inquirers."

## Chapter 34

Returning from the university, Merlin and Cass report to Professor Hamlock. "Professor. It appears that Professor Mundez gathered a small group of scientists to steal your research notes and equipment for their own use. Their strategy was to hijack everything while reporting to the university that their efforts failed to produce anything. Apparently Mundez somehow smuggled information out before his dematerialization."

Professor Hamlock took in Merlin's report, thought a few moments and said, "We will have to establish a security perimeter around the estate and place controls on all communications. I think we will also have to neutralize the observation point on the overlooking stand of trees that was Mundez's favorite haunt. Summon the Gods and Cass, to my quarters in the sub-basement, for a strategy session."

Looking over the assembled Gods and Cass, Hamlock presents the reason for their presence. "We have a problem. Professor Mundez has compromised our very existence. Athena, you will need to put in place a reinforced line of security around the property. We will create additional staff to man observation points and establish a secure line of communication to the game room. Artemis, you will gather the wild animals to be outer sentries and scare off intruders. If the intruders cannot be scared off, members of the outer security circle will report to the observers of the inner circle to relay information on the intruders to the game room.

Cass I want you to review the security plan and make recommendations to Merlin and myself regarding any potential changes needed. Nicole. You and your group will assist Merlin and myself in the game room to help in the staff's expansion. Aphrodite and Persephone, you will control the communications in and out of our home. All suggestions and recommendations to improve our situation should come straight to Merlin and myself. We all know how ruthless Mundez was, so consider this potential group of intruders to be as bad or even worse. Do not over extend yourselves, and be careful. I want everyone to start work preparations now. We cannot afford to be taken by surprise. Everyone, off to your assigned stations."

After everyone leaves, Professor Hamlock talks to Merlin, "Do you know how many are involved, their names and areas of expertise?"

"Most, but not all. They were gathered with Professor Smith in meeting room No. 1, a small conference room at the university and they were easily observed. Most are thinking that an imposter of Professor Mundez was relaying information but they did not indicate how. The information was funneled through Professor Smith who thought the information was ludicrous, but the rewards substantial enough to warrant investigation. Cass and myself will return to the university and further investigate this reprehensible group. Cass can easily infiltrate this nefarious gang and wheedle out their plans and goals."

**Chapter 35**

Professor Hamlock easily creates a university Facilities Engineer, I.D. card for Cass, to enable her access to all departments and rooms. Cass wearing a business suit, glasses and carrying an electronic tablet, locates and follows a professor she recognized from the group she observed the preceding day. She watches his daily routine and overhears many of his cell phone calls. When, after tiring of her surveillance's poor results, and ready to return to the mansion, she hears her target say, "Yes Professor Smith. I will attend the meeting tonight. Yes, I understand, Eight O'clock tonight in meeting room No. 3 at the science department." *Finally,* she thinks.

Breaking off the surveillance, she heads toward the science building. Finding meeting room No. 3 Cass checks all the accesses and spaces available to observe and listen to tonight's meeting. She locates a janitorial closet that will allow a complete view of the conference table and chairs through a slightly opened door.

After checking that all janitorial service is completed for the day, Cass settles in the closet, which has a second door that opens to a hallway separating two meeting rooms. Rearranging the mops, push brooms and buckets, she makes space for a comfortable chair. A wireless bug under the conference table is matched to the High Definition Video Camera sitting on a folding shelf attached to the chair. Sitting back, Cass relaxes in the darkness of the closet.

Professor Smith is the first to arrive. After adjusting the thermostat, he sits at the head of the table. Eight other men immediately follow to sit at the table. A young woman enters the room to fill the glasses, and then after placing the pitcher of ice water on a trivet, on the sideboard, leaves. "Harold, lock the door." Said Professor Smith. "Bart, what is your report?"

"Well, John. We have discovered the security around the Old Hamlock estate has been upgraded. The wooded hill overlooking the property has been sealed off to any foot or vehicle traffic. We will have to locate another suitable observation location. As an alternative, I have been thinking we may have to place visual and audio bugs within the mansion. A warrant to inspect property will not work, but how would an access warrant to update the property value be. Tom's brother is the County Treasurer and could easily provide us with a Warrant of Access for structure and personal property valuation." "What do you think, Tom?"

"Hell yes. Dale has done this for others. This can be done under the guise of fairness with the other property owners in the section. When would you want it?" Said Tom.

"Right away," said John. "Dick, what have you came up with concerning the identity of our informant on the property?"

## Chapter 36

"We cannot find out anything. The man sounds and talks like Mundez. All his referenced information seems accurate, but the fact is Mundez is dead. There are no male relatives in the university or government records. Everything we look at is a dead end. This whole deal with Hamlock and Mundez is a puzzle. We do have information on Miss Dorms and her three friends, the four of whom are students here at the university. There is also a man referred to as Merlin living at the mansion. There is no information on him anywhere. We don't know if his name is an alias or a nick name, and we have a lot of feelers out trying to nail his information down."

"Don. What do you have?"

"I have been pursuing the paper trail on Hamlock's finances. There are no records of material purchases, contractor's billings or building permits for that piece of property. We did find a record of purchase for unimproved land and later, a request for inspection of an finished building which led to an evaluation for tax purposes."

"That should be our reason for a warrant. Bill, Gary and Ron. You three make inquiries. Find out anything you can. Talk to Hamlock's old students. Go to the faculty restaurant and talk to other professors and their assistants. Do not be too aggressive with your questions, but ask what they know about Hamlock's mansion, what he said in and out of the class room," said Smith. "Are there any other reports? If not we will meet again one week from now, here in room No. 3. No. 1 is just too small for us, and we are more comfortable here with a young nice looking science student to see to our needs."

Cass carefully closes the door facing the conference room, quietly turns and opens the door to the hallway. *I have to get back to Professor Hamlock.*

**Chapter 37**

Cass returns to the mansion, and finds the professor in the dining room. "Professor Hamlock, I think we may be in trouble." Showing him what she recorded on the video camera she said, "Can we do anything?"

"We have nothing to worry about. I have prepared signed receipts for all the records that would normally be in the Recorder of Deeds and Tax offices. I will show you where they are filed. I will not be able to present them, but you can as the current property owner. There is also a U.S. Government waiver of all local, state and federal taxes, warrants or inspections due to classified work involving national security. You can show the documents, but they cannot take them, or copy them due to the sensitive nature of the research. We can move the files from my office to the household safe in the library. I will also have to inform Merlin of this development. He needs to be kept up to date on everything. Eat something, and take a break, while I find Merlin. We need to make some documents to account for him being here. Like a complete name, birth certificate and an occupation."

Finding Merlin in the game room, Professor Hamlock brings him up to date and what is needed to legalize his presence and citizenship. Merlin passes on information received from the security perimeters. "Artemis' hounds from hell have scared off three different attempts to penetrate our security. While the backs of some trousers have been ripped and people occasionally knocked out of trees, no one has been hurt. I doubt if there will be any reports to the authorities since they were trespassing. Artemis did have a good laugh when a dog knocked down one of the intruders and slobbered on his face. The man soiled his pants. I think the dog weighed as much as the man."

"It's good that everyone is getting some enjoyment out of a tense situation. Pass this story around to everyone; it will help to keep everyone alert. There have been several attempts to contact Mundez, or rather someone they believe is their informant. Little do they know how misguided their intelligence is. I want everyone to get a good eight hours sleep every twenty-four hours. The kitchen staff is operating twelve hours on and twelve hours off shifts to keep the dining room open twenty-four seven. I think we will put Cass, Persephone and Athena into play, as a disruptive tactic. I have viewed the video Cass made and have identified our adversaries. Also, I have made a list of their home and office addresses, along with telephone numbers and email addresses. Merlin, I must go now to prepare your documentation. When you are done advising the others, come to the library where we will start making your new identity."

Professor Hamlock goes to the library and Merlin goes to find all the other players.

## Chapter 38

Cass and the gods are seated around Merlin listening to Professor Hamlock. "Cass, Athena and Persephone will each identify a target, contact them by telephone or email, and identify themselves as the contact the targets are seeking, asking to set up a meeting. When they meet, they will charm the men, as they well know how, into believing that Merlin, whose real name is George Orwell, is the leader of the cons.

He is preparing to clean out the mansion of everything; equipment to make diamonds from coal, jewels from sand, dirt and scrap metals, to sell to the highest foreign bidder. Once they convince their first targets, they will move to their second targets. I think, that once the girls muddle the minds of these poor men, they will believe anything. The disinformation should bring about the urgency needed to request that the authorities intercede before everything is stolen away. Our documentation will prove to the authorities that his gang of imbeciles is not to be taken seriously and prevent any further attempts of intrusion on their part. It should also set a precedent on which to base an order of protection request. I think that the discredited Professor Smith will be asked to resign from his position from the university and he will go without protest."

Aphrodite could not contain her excitement. "I want to go too. We can rehearse our strategy together. If we study them first, we can determine if and who might be harder to convince and we can gang up on the tough sells. Listen to that, I'm sounding just like those college girls. Merlin, tell the professor how good I can be convincing people of new thoughts."

Merlin smiled and nodded to Hamlock. "Yes, Aphrodite can be very convincing when she sets her mind to it. I would advise you to include her in this espionage ring of beauties."

Hamlock raises one eyebrow and says, "Aphrodite, what do you expect to gain from your participation?"

"Experience, interaction and yes, a little fun. This would be exercising and stretching my mind. I think my capabilities include making a male mortal believe what I want him to believe."

"Very well Aphrodite. You are included, but you must behave yourself. Self-serving pleasures will not be tolerated. When you return, you will tell me what has been learned and how you will use this new knowledge to integrate yourself into this modern society."

"Thank you Professor. You will not regret your decision. Now I will have to decide what to wear."

"Merlin, I want you to arrange the meetings between these men and our agents of *femme fatales* in a manner to prevent suspicion."

"I will start right away." Merlin leaves, and the gods with Cass sit at a large table to discuss their tactics over snacks. Clothes and make up is the main thrust of the conversation. Their discussion is peppered with giggles and an occasional sinister girly laugh.

**Chapter 39**

Cass approached Professor Smith at their pre-arranged meeting place, a hang out for the younger professors. She smiled with what she hoped was a sensual look. "Professor Smith?"

"Yes. And you are?"

"I am the one that called you to this meeting. From what I have overheard around the campus, you are interested in what goes on in Professor Hamlock's mansion. I was his lab assistant before he passed away and now work for Merlin. You would be highly interested in what has been done in the basement. But first, you will have to tell me how will I be compensated for my information?"

"Well, I guess that depends on what you have and how valuable it is. What is your name?"

"Does unlimited gold, silver, diamonds and other precious stones sound valuable? I have no name."

Smith steadied his breathing and trying to control his heartbeat from this information, then calmly said, "I think we can accommodate whatever you want. You will have to tell me in what manner you want to be rewarded and when will you be available for signing an affidavit or a deposition, concerning the information."

"I want one million dollars deposited in an off shore account and I will not sign any documents. My name is to be kept out of this. We are not dealing with an ice cream social group of people. Merlin and his syndicate are murderers, not boy scouts."

"I see. Then I will have to pay you a little less if you are not willing to testify or write down your account of what transpired. I will give you $100,000 now and another $400,000 when your information bears fruit. I am prepared to write you a check now."

"No checks. I will need cash. I can give you a little teaser now, with full information at eight a.m. tomorrow morning at the collegiate coffee shop. No recorders, but I'll talk slow so you can write down the information. I also have the real names of Merlin and his gangsters."

"Agreed. Eight a.m. tomorrow morning at the coffee shop." *And I'll have my digital voice recorder on me, and you under surveillance my beauty. I'll have you for my bidding, and enjoyment.*

"Tomorrow then."

Getting back to the mansion, Cass told Professor Hamlock and Merlin everything that was said. Hamlock said, "He will have some kind of recording device with him and probably someone to watch and follow you. You will have to carry a frequency disrupter on you, and Merlin will see to it that you are not followed."

Cass arrives at seven thirty a.m. finding the coffee shop fairly crowded. She is surprised to see Smith already seated at a corner table. Turning on the frequency disrupter device in her coat pocket, she strolls over to him. "Good Morning professor."

"Good morning young lady."

"Do you have my money?"

"Yes." Said Smith, pulling up a folded manila envelope from his inner coat pocket, sitting it on the table and patting it, while he squeezed the recorder switch with his other hand. Smiling as his thoughts follow his roving eyes when Cass contorts to remove her coat, fantasies holds his full attention. Cass smiles back as if she welcomes his obvious thoughts.

Pushing the envelope toward the table center, Smith said, "Should we get started. I brought pen and paper." He then pulls a note pad and ballpoint pen from his other coat pocket.

Cass reaches for the envelope. Smith quickly stops her with his hand on top of hers. "Not until you tell me what you know.

Cass pulls back her hand from his while swallowing her revulsion as his thoughts transmit through the hand touch. "Fine, then let's start. Merlin's real name is George Orwell. Here is a list of his henchmen's names. I thought writing down the names would be more expedient that reciting them and correcting your spelling. The laboratory is in the basement. The equipment is being boxed up for shipment in a week. There are file cabinets full of research papers and operating manuals. The equipment will produce gold and silver from raw metal ores and chemicals. Other machines will make diamonds and other precious jewels from an assortment of raw materials. There are motors, pumps, hydraulic circuits and high output electrical generators. I saw only Professor Hamlock refer to the manuals and papers that he kept under lock and key. As his lab assistant, I watched the process and retrieved what he needed, tools, materials, coffee and food."

"What did he do with the finished products?"

"I don't know. A truck came weekly to pick up what was available and drop off bags of money he used to pay the government bribes and what is needed to maintain the place. He has a large workforce of slaves, mostly from human traffickers, and some hired staff. They are all under Merlin's control now. His goons watch everyone constantly. Some of the outspoken workers have disappeared and not heard from since. They just disappeared with all their meager belongings."

"How are you free to go where you please?"

Cass looks around as if to see if anyone is watching, then crosses her legs and raises her dress to show an electronic ankle bracelet. "This is how. I am taking a break from doing errands. If I stray too far, the bracelet is supposed to give me a fatal shock. They do not know that I designed this unit and know how to manipulate it. They expect me to return shortly and service one or more of those ugly thugs. They are rewarded with the women household staff's company, for good work and loyalty to Merlin. With this money, I will be able to escape and with your knowledge of what is happening, you can convince the authorities to stop them."

*Yes, I will stop them and take over the operation and you my dear will be one of my many companions.*

"You can have full faith that I will get them jailed and release your friends from their awful situation."

"Here is the electronic address and my account number to deposit the rest of the money." Reaching for the envelope, Cass picks it up and places it in her purse. "Is what I told you enough?"

"Is there anything else you can tell me?"

"No, not that I can think of now, but I can contact you if I remember anything else."

"Then yes, you did good. Where will you go now?"

"I would rather not say, but be assured it will be a safe place for me. I must leave now or they will become suspicious and hunt me down if I am gone too long and their interrogations can become very painful".

"Go my dear and be very careful. Do you need any assistance returning?"

"No. My car may be under surveillance." Getting up to leave, Cass identifies a member of Smith's group, watching from a table across the café.

Merlin, in disguise, is sitting at the counter and nods at one of the male household staff sitting at a table. He gets up and carries a tray with the remnants of his order. He trips himself throwing the tray and it's contents over Smith's assistant. An argument ensues while the staff member attempts to wipe off the debris while the observer tries escaping to follow Cass, who makes a successful get-a-way.

Merlin continues to enjoy his coffee and donuts with a satisfied smile while the two men recover. Smith's anger is evident while the observer shrugs with hopelessness. They leave the café with growls of discontent. Waiting a few minutes until the two men leave the area, Merlin then returns to the mansion.

# Chapter 40

Athena has made contact with Harold, one of Professor Smith's men, and sets up a meeting with him at the public library, 6 p.m. tonight. She is wearing a low cut frilly blouse, a mini skirt and high heel shoes. She had not told Harold her name, but did describe herself in an understated manner, telling him she would stand out from the other library patrons.

Harold entered the library and noticed that all eyes are looking in the same direction. As he cleared the entrance foyer, he realized why. Athena sits at a table, legs crossed, leaning over to read from a world atlas of the ancient time. Noticing Harold's entrance, she stood and leaned over, as if to better see the upper part of the page. The view of Athena's cleavage and stretched out legs pulling up her skirt took his breath away. He had forgotten why he is there, stood transfixed. An entering patron bumps into him, bringing about a clearing of the mind and to his purpose there.

Athena raised her eyes to Harold's making his heart skip a few beats. He approached Athena and asks, "Are you waiting for someone?"

"Yes, a man named Harold."

"I am Harold. May I sit down?"

"Yes." Said Athena, closing the large atlas and pushing it aside.

"Do you have some information for me?"

"Yes I do. Very valuable information."

"Can I have your name?"

"No, you do not need my name. Are you able to finalize any arrangement we decide on here, tonight?"

"Yes. I am fully empowered to complete any financial dealing we agree to. It would help if I can verify who you are, the information you have, and how you came into acquiring your information."

"You do not need my name as I will only deal in cash. I will give you the information a little at a time, to incrementally increase what you will pay me, as you realize the accumulating worth. I have this information because, as a server in Professor Hamlock's mansion, I would overhear his planning and discussions of building, maintaining and operating his equipment, and his negotiations over what he made. I also performed the same duties, after the professor passed away, with Merlin and his men. Now, what is your starting bid and what do you want to know about first?"

Harold was taken aback at her bluntness and stammered. "We will start off with some information that will allow me to set a starting bid."

"Good. Professor Hamlock invented gadgets that could make gold and silver from scrap metals and a few minerals."

"I think that should be worth $150,000."

"He also had machinery that would create any jewels you can imagine, made from sand and other cheap materials."

"$250,000."

"I can tell you where the equipment is stored."

"$300,000."

"I can give you the location of all his research notes, blueprints and schematics, maintenance and operational manuals."

"$400,000."

"I can tell you how to acquire all this, his distribution methods and buyers for his products. Also, I have detailed blueprints of the mansion, security procedures and schedules of Merlin and his men, with a listing of all their names."

"$500.000."

"Good. Now make that an even million dollars and we have a deal."

"How will I be able to verify the information?"

"You already have the verification. I have confirmed this by your questions asked around the campus. How is this? I will pass you portions of the information; say twenty percent at a time as you pay me $200,000 on the receipt of each portion. As I said before, cash only."

*This gal is not only gorgeous, but also smart as hell. I wonder if Smith will give her to me when this is all done. I understand that the mansion is loaded with rooms where I could keep her. Talk about a Star Trek Fantasy Deck!* "Sure. We can do this. Where do you want our next meet?"

"Right here. Same table, same time tomorrow."

The next evening Harold is waiting for Athena. An envelope, stuffed with cut paper, bulges out his coat pocket. He is nervously waiting, constantly checking his watch, and then looking at the entrance door. Athena arrives with a flurry of attention. Men try to out-distance each other to open the door for her. A sultry smile rewards the small group trying to reach the door first. Each man tries to out maneuver each other for the door handle and her attention. Her thank you warms the air as she walks past. Her every facet is memorized by the befuddled group. Business cards and scraps of paper hurriedly scribbled with telephone numbers are ignored.

Athena spots Harold and starts toward him with a killer walk, carrying a large valise. She sits, and then asked, "Did you bring my money? I need to arrange my transportation out of this burg."

"Yes, I have it right here." Said Harold, patting his bulged pocket.

"How much?"

"$200,000. As we agreed on."

"Good. Here are the plans on the machinery," said Athena, sliding an 8 x 10 manila envelope across the table."

"Did you bring the other information with you?"

"Do you have the rest of the money?"

"Yes. We can conclude this exchange if you want."

"Fine with me.

"Can I have it?"

"After I get mine first. Put it on the table."

Harold pulls out a thicker envelope from his other pocket and sets it on the table in front of him.

"I have everything you need and want right here."

"Do I need to count it? How can I be sure you're trustworthy?"

"You can trust me. If not, you know where you can find me."

They slide their packets across the table as the same time. Concluding their exchange, they both stood up to leave, Athena toward the main entrance, and Harold toward a small side door. Leaving the Library, Athena quickly jumps into a car that quietly pulls up to the curb.

"How did it go?" Asks Merlin.

"Fine, but I think he stiffed me from the feel of these envelopes." Then opening the first envelope Athena looks at the cut paper. Opening the second envelope produced the same result.

"That's O.K." Said Merlin. This was set up just to give him information that they cannot use. You did good. Let's get back to the mansion. First I'll have to ditch the car that is following me."

At the second stoplight, Austin cut off the car following Merlin and Athena. Austin, slightly bumping the front of the car, waited for the driver to get out to check for damage before he pulled away with a heavy throttle. When they all returned to the mansion, and reported to Professor Hamlock, he chuckled at the information. "Aphrodite is up next. I don't think we will have to pursue this any further. They are already sold on the intelligence they received.

## Chapter 41

Aphrodite contacted Ron at the home of his Mistress. "Ron, this is Merlin's girlfriend. I want to meet with you. I have information for you."

"How did you get this number?"

"Come on, you can't be serious. Everybody knows that you are shacking up with that bimbo. Meet with me and you will not regret it."

"Who is this again?"

"Don't play dumb with me lover boy. I have the information that your whole group is looking for. The whole campus knows what is going on. Your guys are not too selective with what they say and to whom. You people really need to secure your meeting places before blabbing everything out to the world."

"Alright, but Irma is not a bimbo. If you want to deal with me, you are going to have to be a little more respectful."

"O.K. I'll call someone else with the information. Maybe the University Provost will be more interested in this info than you are. What do you think?"

"No. No. You're talking to me already. Why make it harder on you? Why don't we meet at the Swan Lake over on north campus tonight at 8 p.m.?"

"Do you think I'm stupid? We'll meet at the Donut Shop just off North Drive at 6:30 tonight. I don't think I can trust you at that isolated Swan Lake. I have all the information you have been asking about on campus. Do you have a price in mind for it?"

"No. Do you?"

"I was thinking of around $500,000. That is a very cheap price. You would reach a break-even point in a couple of days."

"That's a little steep. There's not much of a money flow right now. How about $250,000?"

"Bullshit. The information is worth at least a couple of million. Just bring the money tonight. I know that your organization is loaded. I have done my homework. Now it's your turn to deal."

Aphrodite is dressed in a clinging cream-colored dress sitting at café table, a cup of coffee and a donut sitting in front of her. She has a four-foot long, eight-inch diameter cardboard tube hanging on her chair. Her legs are pulled back to the side of the chair, crossed at the ankles. Her posture, clothes and smile ooze sensuality. Her eyes screamed sex. The dimmed lighting accentuates her smoldering look.

Ron enters the cafe door, walks a few steps, and then steps back when he notices Aphrodite. His smile lights the path before him. Approaching the table he asks, "Are you waiting for Ron?"

"Yes, are you lucky Ron?"

"Yes I am, Ron that is. May I sit down?"

"Yes, not unless you want to talk standing up."

Sitting, Ron decides the woman sitting across from him is more beautiful than anyone he has ever met. Aphrodite stretches her hand across the table to cover Ron's hand.

"I hope you have everything I want. Do you?"

"I think so," stuttered Ron.

"Good, then let's get started." Pushing a sheet of paper across the table Aphrodite said, "This is a list of material things that I can provide you. I don't think a list of non-material things I could provide would be appropriate until I receive my money." Aphrodite removed her hand from his.

Ron swallows hard. Little beads of sweat form on his head, armpits and groin. "Irma is just a friend of mine. She is nothing special in my life."

"I know," said Aphrodite. "It's just that your wife doesn't understand you and your needs."

"Yes, something like that. Yes, I have brought the money and I'm hoping we can conclude our business tonight, or rather before tomorrow morning."

"Are you wanting to negotiate with me all night?"

"I was thinking something like that." Ron reviews the long list of information she is positioned to reveal to him. "Is everything in that tube on the chair?"

"Yes with verification references. The operation can be taken over with very few minutes lost in the transfer. It would not even be a blip on the time schedule. Again, is my money ready and in cash?"

"Yes." Ron places an envelope on the table, but keeps his hand covering it.

Aphrodite pulls the tube off the chair back and places it on the table. "Do you have a room close by, or do I need to shop around for a hotel?"

"Yes, I have a suite at the Imperial."

"First class. Good. Give me the telephone and suite number, and give me a few minutes to get there."

"I thought we could go together."

226

"No, I want to come back in my own transportation. I'll meet you there in thirty minutes. You can, Hhhmmmmm, freshen up and chill a bottle to celebrate the deal."

Ron pulls out a business card and writes down the telephone and suite number before passing it over to Aphrodite.

"You can leave first, I don't want us to be seen leaving together, just in case Merlin is having me watched."

"But."

"No. You first."

Ron picks up the tube and leaves first while Aphrodite finishes her coffee and donut. Walking out she opens the passenger door of Merlin's car. "That went nice. Is the money O.K.?"

"What do you think? I threw it into the trash can on my way out."

"I feel that the professor will be extremely happy with the success of his plans. We had better get back and report to him."

## Chapter 42

Professor Hamlock gathered Merlin, Cass and the Gods. "I have not received word from any of my contacts, that Professor Smith contacted any government authority for warrants gaining access to our property. I am thinking that they may be planning to come in force to physically overwhelm us and take over their presumed idea of what our estate security entails. It would be prudent for us to change our strategy.

Merlin. Cass. We should call on what others would see as supernatural beings. We'll redecorate the basement and hide the entrance to the game room. Cass, go to the basement and make it look somewhat like the game room. Merlin, we will convert the door to the game room to look like book shelving. Then we will conjure up some spirits to greet any unwanted guests we may encounter. What do you think Merlin? Did you have ghosts from the graves, demons and such in your time?"

"Yes we did. And, I can see what you are thinking. We can re-create a dungeon of horrors to entertain unwelcomed visitors." Merlin had a hearty laugh. A laugh like none he has had in many centuries.

After changing the game room door to a sliding book shelving unit, Hamlock and Merlin start planning on what mythical, and some new entities, to re-create. Ghost, dragons, apparitions, vampires, giant spiders, rooms and things that devour people, and endless creatures of mayhem were planned and designed.

Merlin favored a medieval torture dungeon replenished with mythical creatures that delivers justice and retribution. A maze that is inescapable and filled with monsters that materialized from the ground, air and maze structures itself is planned, designed and created. Outer and inner rings of security is redone and manned by created creatures. Internal security is build into the air itself. Merlin is like a kid in a candy shop. Laughing while seeing situations form in his mind like a normal person setting up a detailed planned Halloween celebration. Hamlock also is enjoying himself, referring to old books on spirits of old.

A cemetery was created behind the mansion between the woods and garden. Mausoleums, crypts, disturbed and open graves were generously spread. Living dead were strategically placed laying in-wait. When all was done and ready, Professor Hamlock gathered everyone to the dining room. The household staff joined in the festivities and banquet. Everyone more or less served themselves from the side tables surrounding the room. Laughter and spirited conversation encompassed all while describing what was done and what is expected to happen. Alternate plans were discussed and placed into effect.

As the pitch of the celebration diminished, a bell warning of a security breach was sounded. A General Quarters type of announcement is made and everyone goes to pre-determined places of action.

**Chapter 43**

Video cameras stream live images to the game room where Professor Hamlock, Merlin, Cass, Gods and the four Geeks observe the monitors. Scores of men are descending from the wooded knoll overlooking the mansion. An eerie glowing fog grows out of the valley between the knoll and the mansion then suddenly spits out mounted horses with riders swinging weapons of ancient warriors. Blood curdling screams echo up the hillside. The descending men stop in their tracks, not believing what they see. Shooting the apparitions does not stop or slow them down.

Some of the intruders turn and run, while others run backwards, back up they hill. They discover that a twenty-foot deep trench, that they all are forced into, blocks their retreat. Barbarians materialize to crowd the men down the trench through a cavern opening into a dungeon of horror. Cries of tortured souls echo in this chamber of terror, turning blood into ice water flowing within the veins of these hunters turned victims. A barred door, opening into a large cell, screeches open and the frightened men are herded inside. Tools and equipment of torture, covered in blood, are situated around the room surrounded by cells. Body parts are hanging from hooks suspended on chains from the darkness of the ceiling.

Some of the men are crying while the remaining stand mute in a daze, not understanding what they are seeing. Some are making fearful noises as they view the horrific scene taking place. From somewhere high in the darkness above them, a door opens and bangs against a solid stop. Heavy footsteps are heard slowly descending the rock steps. Loud breathing, accentuated by throaty grunts, is spewed out as the footsteps draw nearer.

Most of the confined men squeeze to the back of the cell, the farthest distance from the barred door, trying to mentally remove themselves from the nightmares seen in their minds. The men that do not move to the back of the cell are catatonic in their stance and not really aware of what the scene is unfolding before them. A powerful laugh from hell echoes through the chamber, followed by "Who will be the first to taste my blade and feed Hades."

Many of the men lose weight from the release of excretions and body fluids that slowly snake down their pant legs. The center of the cell floor slowly begins to open, the abyss mouth creeping outward toward the cell walls. All eventually plunge into the gaping black hole. Consciousness leaves them as they fall into the unknown.

The designers of this confrontation congratulate themselves on their accomplishment. Their attention is now drawn to a different monitor screen showing a smaller group of men leaving the safety of the woods, approaching the cemetery that borders on the garden. As they cross over the graveyard's perimeter, they stop. An apparition stumbles out of a crumbling mausoleum door and falls to the ground.

Growling, the body, with its rotted funeral clothing falling away, rises to a semi crouch, turns to face the men, and staggers toward them. Eyes wide and mouths open, they are dumbfounded. Their minds retrieve scenes from horror movies seen in their youth. Shots from automatic weapons ring out as they try to stop this corpse from the past. The apparition continues toward them. A mist, florescent from the full moon, rises from the cemetery surface. Groans and moans come from the charged atmosphere. A group of dead cadavers, partially dressed in decayed clothing, clumsily approaches them. More shots ring out to no avail. The dead carcasses outflank and surround the men, who are rooted to the ground, and then are slowly driven into the glowing mist.

The smell of rotting flesh spur the captives forward. The men at the rear of the moving group hear screams from the front. Blindly shuffling through the thick mist, the men fall like an army marching over a cliff edge to their doom. Primal screams of eminent death are stopped mid utterance. Again, congratulations are offered and received. The geeks high five each other, while Merlin, Cass and the Gods look at their actions with non-recognition. The action of a 'High five' is completely foreign to them.

The monitors show still another group of men coming in a frontal assault to the mansion. They had raced down the driveway toward the main entrance in SUVs. Their caravan is stopped as though they encountered a brick wall. The second vehicle striking the first, and the third striking the second, and so on until all ten vehicles are wrecked. The occupants fall out and gather their senses. Weapons in hand, they cautiously approach the invisible wall, feeling for any obstruction with their hands. Coming to the invisible barrier, a dense fog descends over them.

They can hear heavy gunfire all around them. Explosions surround them with dirt and debris falling like rain. The fog lifts with wafts floating ten feet above the ground surface. Approaching soldiers are wearing gas masks and carry antique rifles with bayonets attached. The explosions around them start to boil up with a yellow mist. "Oh my God. Poison gas. Quick, jump into the craters. Protect yourselves," yells one of their leaders. The gas, heavier than air, slowly descends to smother and suffocate. The last visions of the intruders are the bayonets raised for a thrusting penetration.

The first group of men dispatched from the dungeon wake up in a plowed field that extends beyond their vision. Disorientated and groggy, they stir in stunned disbelief. The sun is rising over the horizon, lighting a land unknown to them. They stand as a group and slowly walk toward the sun. The second group, from the cemetery, awakens with birds screaming and singing, within a jungle surrounding them. There is a swampy, backwater slew behind them and a broad path through the jungle in front. Knowing that they had to go somewhere, they stood and start walking down the jungle path.

The third group of men from the battlefield find themselves in a stubble field where farm workers are cutting straw with scythes, in a foreign country where they cannot understand the language. All three groups are unharmed and unarmed.

The defenders of the mansion are carefully reviewing the monitor recordings for the presence of Professor Smith. Smith is safely seated in his office, by a cell phone waiting for word that his planned operation is successful. A GPS type instrument is used to locate his physical presence. Professor Hamlock and Merlin again start up equipment in the game room.

A new entity is created and materializes just behind Smith. Feeling an ominous presence in the room with him, he tries to mentally rid himself of the goose bumps covering his body. Slowly turning in his chair a red slime slowly settles over his face from the large mouth of a creature too horrible to really describe, other than the large pointed teeth sprouted out of a bloody mouth surrounded by a grotesque green mold covered face. Its breath is eye watering and unlike anything Smith had ever encountered. The creature bends over to pick Smith up in a bear hug. It gives him a face-covering kiss that extends ear to ear. Smith believes the creature is going to eat his head, and holds his breath for the inevitable end of his life. The kiss lingers long enough for Smith to think he is going to suffocate from the slobbery kiss. He cannot believe the stench and is trying to quickly formulate a plan to save his life. The creature releases his kiss when Smith suddenly realizes that the creature is sexually aroused. His screams diminish into sobs, and then become silent in the throes of the creatures lust.

## Chapter 44

"I think we are done," said Professor Hamlock. "Merlin, do you have anything to say?"

"We finally came together as a team. This shows we can all come together to accomplish a common goal. We have to continue with this cooperation and singular focus."

Aphrodite said with a smile, "I believe we all had fun. I know that I can fully function and interact with mortals. Flirting with that man Ron gives me new hope to fulfill my desires in this time. I thought my time spent here would have to be a celibate existence. Now I know better. I am ready to become a mortal."

"You will have to acquire marketable skills in order to have an income, other than the skills you are known for," whispered Nicole out loud to herself. Noticing that everyone heard her comment she told the gathering, "I'm sorry. I did not mean that. Aphrodite has proven herself and I have yet to catch up on her new outlook."

"That is alright Nicole, I knew what you really meant," replies Aphrodite.

Professor Hamlock, looking proud of his fellow combatants, said, "I think champagne is in order. We should go to the dining area to celebrate our final triumph. Come along."

As the celebration carries into the night, Merlin observes that the gods are indeed becoming more human like. He notices that the female gods have had too much to drink. Their voices are slurred and eyes drooping. He comments to the professor. "They all have had too much to drink. Should I have the servers stop serving them?"

"Let them have their fun Merlin. They deserve to enjoy themselves and to realize a lesson learned on waking in the morning. I don't think that they have experienced a hang over yet and it will be interesting how they react to it," said Hamlock with a laugh.

Aphrodite remembered that her favorite food is ice cream and orders some, not knowing of her stomach's reaction to the mix with champagne. Dyllan walks up to Aphrodite. "If I did not know better, I would think you are pregnant."

"What would make you think that?" replied Aphrodite.

"Ice cream is one of the foods that mortals crave when they are pregnant. I wouldn't eat too much of that."

"Why? I enjoy it very much."

"Drinking alcoholic beverages and eating ice cream together will usually make one sick to their stomach."

Aphrodite stops eating. Looking at Dyllan, she says "Really."

"Yes, really."

"I have so much to learn. Can we sit tomorrow and talk about all the other peculiarities' common to mortal living?"

"Learning what is peculiar to others is a life long endeavor. Everyone is different, and reacts differently. One never stops learning until the day they die."

"So there is not hope for me?" Complained Aphrodite.

"As much hope as the rest of humanity."

"I wish knowledge was like food, where you could just eat it to learn it."

"Ask the professor. Maybe he can come up with something novel to accommodate you."

Merlin, seeing the sobriety of the group rapidly deteriorating, mentioned to Hamlock. "We need to get everyone off to bed, or it will take days for them to recuperate."

"I agree. There will be a lot of cleaning up to do tomorrow and the kids will have classes to attend at the university. We will also have to come up with a story to leak out to cover what happened tonight. That will take some time to think of."

## Chapter 45

Early morning is greeted with birds singing in bright sunshine. The aromatic smell of coffee and a menu of breakfast foods being prepared for Hamlock's guests to order fill the mansion. Places are being set on the huge dining table and everything is brought to readiness. The first to arrive is Merlin, followed by Professor Hamlock. Merlin, following his morning inspection routine, nods his head in approval while Hamlock sits opposite of Merlin. Their breakfast is served to them the same as always, coffee, a fruit juice, oatmeal and heavy cream, eggs and sausage. Looking across the table to Merlin, Hamlock said, "How long do you think we can continue eating like this before we start suffering from obesity?"

"Not soon I hope. I would hate to return to the days of gruel and congealed animal fat on cold bread.

Even the blood pudding from my distant past leaves a distasteful memory. Eggs, if available, would be used to disguise the odor and trick taste buds on the tongue."

"Merlin, please, our food has been served. Why must you ruin what we will soon enjoy?"

"Sorry."

Cass enters the room and sits at her place of the table. Her breakfast is a more modest selection. Juice, toast, bacon and eggs are served to her. "I don't know how you two can drink and eat what you do. The foods you are addicted to will kill you. I have to work hard to counter what little I eat."

The gods enter as a group, excitedly talking to each other at the same time. From the tone of their voices they are not suffering the ravages of drinking late into the night. Their volume drowns out the conversation of the earlier arrivals. They order individually. They have not established a routine in their meals. Everyday, they each order food items different from before, as if they have to sample everything, compare notes and decide at a later time, what their favorite foods might be.

The four geeks arrive last with sleep still in their eyes, yawning and fumbling with their clothes. Austin and Travis's hair is still uncombed, their shirts hanging outside their pants and Travis's shoelaces are untied.

246

The two girls, Dyllan and Nicole are a little more presentable but are without makeup. All they order is juice and toast, apparently suffering from the late night alcohol. "Uncle Hamlock. Can we have a driver take us to the university? We are running a little late this morning," said Nicole. Looking at the gods, she frowns and mutters, "Why do they always catch the breaks. They will find out what its like to be human soon enough." Then looking back to the professor, said, " We will catch a ride with someone to get back."

"No," said the professor. "I will have the driver return this afternoon to pick you up. We need to discuss our plans for the future."

"What plans? I thought we would live happily ever after," said Nicole. "After our adventure last night I don't want to venture more than a day at a time into the future. That was just downright creepy, worse than any horror movie I ever saw."

"Yes, but very effective," said Professor Hamlock. "I don't think that we will see anymore interference from the university staff. I have completed identifications for Merlin and the Gods. They now have everything they need to go out into the world and become honorable members of society. I don't think that I have to explain the emphasis on the word honorable, do I?"

Aphrodite looks like she had just been caught with her hand in the cookie jar. "Professor. You are not referring to me I hope?"

"No, I am referring to everyone. We cannot draw attention to ourselves or reveal what we are."

Professor looks around to everyone with a smile. "Merlin and myself are just about done perfecting immortality to our young humans and to you Gods after becoming human."

Artemis looks a little concerned. "I dislike the terminology, 'after becoming human'. That sounds like everyone thinks that we are less than human now. I think that we are more than that. We have a history with lineage. The human population thinks of us as Gods. We are spoken of highly in their literature and mythology. We were and are a force to be reckoned with. We ..." A tear slides down her cheek. "We are nothing in this time. We have to reinvent ourselves to survive, changing our identities and roles in this time. We were held in a position of esteem and now must conform to the norm of today's society. We are now diminished in every respect. Sometimes I feel we would be better off dematerializing to become, as we were, a God of mythology, held in respect and awe. If we cannot exist in our own self-esteem today, even as a human, then we should return to our station in legend as told from Mt. Olympus."

Merlin proclaims, "I feel that having immortality will be good for me. I will not have to worry about being imprisoned in some rock for centuries, dying, waiting for someone like Professor Hamlock to bring me back. I know I'll be able to positively contribute to society. That is all I have ever wanted to do, to make life better for the world. Oh, I believe that I am acclimating to this time. Is this not what you currently state is 'standing on a soap box?'"

Everyone smiles, and Professor Hamlock said, "I think we are all getting into the mainstream of today's mind set."

The group finishes their breakfast, and individually leaves to prepare for the day. The four geeks depart for the university, Merlin to the game room to research his immortality and the Gods to the library to discuss their new roles.

**Chapter 46**

The four geeks arrive at the university to the student body curious about the recent events. Rumors abound about the night before. "We don't know what you are talking about. We did not see or hear anything like what you are saying. There were a couple of burglars that were chased off last night, but nothing is missing. The attempted burglary was reported and nothing incriminating found, so I believe the whole matter has been dropped."

"But what about the missing professors?"

"I have no idea. Maybe you should contact the police to see if a missing person report was filed, or ask the administration if they are on some kind of sabbatical?" Excusing themselves they continued on to the first class.

Professor Hamlock joins Merlin in the Game Room. "Merlin, I think we should engage the Gods to help them in their transition. I hope the confusion of Artemis is not indicative of the other Gods feelings. I also think that I have found a way to give immortality to you and the Gods other than re-creating. After going into the materialization chamber, a temporary reverse engineering followed by a DNA and gene modification to a retuned finalization, should give all of you what you want, human perspectives but with immortality. There are some downfalls, one being able to explain why you do not age like everyone else and two, seeing acquired friends and relatives dying off. Losing people you like and love can be very stressful. It's called survivor syndrome. It is especially prevalent to a sole survivor of a very close-knit group like military or work teams. We will talk of this at length when we have a group discussion with the others."

Aphrodite is lounging in the library deep in thought. Suddenly she looks to the other Gods and expresses what is on her mind. "I think we have been looking at this all wrong. We should be thinking about how to improve our situation. We need to be very critical to what we are doing. We will be here for eternity. Our plans are really long range as opposed to the human's short life span. We won't age, get sick or die. What we do need to worry about is providing for ourselves. An income for eternity is a big deal, and we will not be able to work for money like the humans. Granted, contributing to humanity is a second responsibility, to be taken seriously, but first we have to ensure that we are taken care of. We have to find a way to help each other in order to survive. This will require cooperation and mutual support. Petty differences will no longer be allowed. We are a family, a very unique family of brothers and sisters that take care of each other. We will not be able to rely on the Professor, but still think of him as family. Merlin will also have to be part of our family. I have come to think of the Professor and Merlin as our protectors. They have both proven to have our best interest at heart. I do not think it would be right to bring other gods into our circle and further complicate our situation.

Adonis looks a little sad and said, "I have many friends from Mt. Olympus that would be a joy to have here as friends, but I wonder how well they could adapt to this time. I agree that we should remain as we are."

"Good. If there are no other thoughts on this matter, I will approach the Professor and Merlin to tell them our decision. Maybe the Professor will have suggestions to provide for our future."

Later that evening, after Nicole and her three friends return from the university, Professor Hamlock calls everyone together for a conference. "Aphrodite approached me this afternoon with the Gods concerns over their future, their livelihood and how to manage what lies ahead for them. Merlin and I have discussed this and decided, that is if you all agree, to form a group to continue what I have started here, with everyone, including the household staff, sharing the fruits of our work. We will have to expand our facility to help the impoverished of the world improve their lives.

And Aphrodite thought. *'And where will I start in pursuit of suitors. This time is filled with yummy men just waiting for me'.*

A Glossary of Characters
The Palace of Virtual Reality


Professor Ambrose Hamlock............Uncle of Nicole

Nicole Dorms.....................Niece of Prof. Hamlock

Dyllan.................................Austin's Girlfriend

Austin................................Dyllan's Boyfriend

Travis...................................Nicole's Boyfriend

Merlin..................Magician. First To Be Re-Created

Cass......Prof. Hamlock's Re-created Personal Assistant

Professor Jago Mundez......Prof. Hamlock's Arch Rival

Aphrodite.....................The Greek Goddess of Love

Athena........................................God of War

Adonis..........................God Of Beauty and Desire

Artemis.The Huntress. God Of Nymphs, Dogs And Deer

Persephone............God Of Spring, Plants and Harvest

The Keys

A short story from the book

The Keys
And Other Short Stories

By Charles Schwend

Follows For Your
Enjoyment

Now Available At
Most Major Book Stores
And
Amazon

## The Keys

A board-end suddenly pops up, tripping me while examining my latest purchase. My nostrils fill with the accumulated dust that became airborne when I belly flopped onto the floor. Angry from my clumsiness, I kick the protruding board only to hear a cry of pain coming from me. Hopping on the uninjured foot, I chastised myself for doing this dumb thing. Loosing my balance, my face makes contact with the dust covered attic floor again. Tears flow from my eyes, making craters in the deep residue of time. I remain stretched out on the floor, waiting for the pain to leave my nose, which I just know is was broken.

Sneezing from the dust coating my sinuses cause more extreme pain. Opening my eyes that are looking down into the cavity I see a tangle of golden metal. My eyes focus while pushing up from the floor and I see that the tangle is a ring of brass keys. A mix of large and small, some bright and shiny, some dull with a green patina, some ornately made, some crudely crafted. They are old, very old, and I cannot remember any locks that would accept these ancient artifacts, but I have not examined the basement. I am keeping that experience for last. Reaching in to retrieve my find, I then stand up on unsteady feet.

I slowly descend the steep stairway, hoping to find the water has been turned on. The trickle of blood dripping from my nose will need attention, and my hands and face can use washing. Brushing the dust off my clothes will be fine until I make my way back to the hotel. I think returning in the morning to complete inspecting this once proud mansion would be the right thing to do. Reaching the kitchen, I find some old washcloths and towels.

The plumbing rattles and growls when the faucet is turned on. Smelly brown water gurgles out, followed with clean, fresh smelling water pouring into the sink. Gently I wash away the blood, and then hold the cold wet cloth to my upturned nose. After several applications of the cold, wet water, the pain and bleeding, to my relief, stops.

Returning to my hotel room, I shower and hit the sack early. Dawn's first light finds me searching the basement for a matching lock to a key on the ring. The eeriness, of this supposedly haunted ancient home, makes the hair on my neck stand up, and goose bumps on my arms push out feeling like large grained sand on wet skin. Everything feels like a bad omen, or even a forewarning against my current endeavor.

Relief that I had the foresight to have the power turned on does little to alleviate my pounding heart. Searching this ominous space would be a terrifying experience with only a flashlight to illuminate the secrets hidden in the nooks and crannies of this foreboding place. A door that appears to look like an empty shelving unit reveals itself when turning a corner of the wall. There is no knob or handle, just a finger recess. Little effort is required to swing open the unit, revealing a staircase descending into a dark abyss. A high pitched squeal sounds a warning against trespassers. There is no switch in or outside the doorway, only an oily torch and self-igniting matches, nestled in holders on the wall. Striking a match on the cobbled wall produces a flame to ignite the torch.

At the bottom of the stairs is a massive timbered door with two enormous locks, above and below a huge wooden handle. Two of the keys from the ring, unlock the door. Stuck from years of non-use, the door only opens after great exertion. Cold, damp, and foul air that pushes out from behind the door produces an unearthly howl, bringing a fog like airborne plasma with it. An uncontrollable breath puts me into a temporary trance-like state and leaves me with a sweet, and acidy metallic taste.

The floor at the bottom of the stairs is hidden in a blackened void. Debating with myself whether I should proceed downward is pushed aside with an unexplainable curiosity. My descending footsteps echo to what seems to be infinity. The further I descend, the colder and heavier the air becomes, making my breathing like trying to overcome a soaked blanket covering my face. Niches along the stairway resemble ancient catacomb burial receptacles. The dampness of the air runs down my body in rivulets filling my shoes. I am living a nightmare with no control over my destiny.

The bottom of the stairs that looms ahead rest on moss covered stone blocks partially embedded in a slime covered rock floor. Cautiously stepping out, trying to see what kind of room I have found, a large rectangular space opens to my vision. A large panoramic mural depicting human sacrifices and mass killing of war, is vividly portrayed on the far wall above five doors. The doors are made of timber with barred openings in the upper half. The light from my torch does not penetrate deep enough in the rooms to reveal what they contain.

Deciding to enter the rooms to satisfy my curiosity, I begin with the first room to my left. The first two and the last two rooms are dungeon cells with shackles and drainage trenches that lead to an opening at the bottom of the back walls. The center room appears to be some kind of a storage area, filled with dry rotted wooden boxes with contents that have turned to dust many years before. The boxes at the rear wall had collapsed to reveal another locked, solid timbered door. One of the keys on the ring unlocks the nearly immobile door. The echoes of protesting frozen hinges reverberate through the room. Pushing with all my might slowly cracks the door open an inch at a time. Dank, musty air attacks my sense of smell. I cannot tell if I must sneeze, cry, blow my nose or wipe the tears from my eyes first. A sneeze effectively clears both my nasal passage and my head.

A mind-freezing scene attacks my senses. Through an arched doorway is an adjoining room where sits five skeletons in five thrones; surrounded by chests filled with items of glistening gold and blackened silver, mixed with large multi-colored crystals. There is a sixth, empty throne that is clean as if waiting for an occupant.

Their rotted and shredded clothing hung from bones like grotesque confetti. Long golden rods are still held in clenched fingers and propped up against the thrones back. The slack jaws appear to be grinning at me, teeth stained with age. A light, source unseen, reflects a ghoulish glow on and around the setting. I notice that there are iron shackles chaining a leg bone of each skeleton to rings embedded in the stone floor.

A warning comes to mind, to escape now to the freedom of the outside world. Thinking of the profits that could be made from this mansion and its contents forces me to continue with my investigation. Walking to an open chest of treasure, I pick up a jeweled broach made of solid gold. Forgetting the five occupants of the room, I randomly picked up exquisite pieces of jewelry and ancient coins that looks as if just recently crafted. Time is lost as I continue with my obsession. A deeper chill begins to permeate the room, alerting me to the passage of time. My watch reveals to me that it is now early evening. The whole day has passed without my realization.

The sound of a closing door makes me jump up from a crouch, torturing my cramped muscles. Turning I see the door has slammed shut. Rushing to it I discover it is locked with no key access on this side. Looking around the door to find some kind of release or unlocking mechanism, I see a green brass plate mounted above in the stone. My stomach contents turned to acid as I read the words. "The keeper guardians of my bounty grow by the number of treasure hunters found."

A greenish cloud of gas drops from the ceiling and I slowly slide down the door to the floor. Awakening, I find myself sitting in the sixth throne, next to a new empty seat and I am chained to the floor. A smiling apparition appears and approaches me with a golden rod in its hands. I know that there is no rescue and greed is my downfall.

www.ingramcontent.com/pod-product-compliance
Lightning Source LLC
Chambersburg PA
CBHW070900250626
47159CB00003B/1130